ODYSSEUS II
THE JOURNEY
THROUGH HELL

ODYSSEUS II—THE JOURNEY THROUGH HELL

"Circe, how do we get home from here?" asked Odysseus.

"There's only one person who can tell you that – the prophet Tiresius."

"But he's been dead for hundreds of years!"

"Exactly," said Circe, and unrolled a torn and faded map. "If you want to get home, you must visit the land of the Dead."

It had taken ten, long, terror-filled years for the Greeks to win the Trojan War and now, Odysseus, their victorious leader, wanted nothing more than to return home to his wife and son.

What he didn't know was that the voyage ahead would be more terrible than anything he had yet encountered and the journey through Hell was just the beginning . . .

ABOUT THE AUTHORS

Tony Robinson plays the character Baldrick in the television series "The Black Adder" and performs and co-writes "Tales from Fat Tulip's Garden" for Central Television. He attended the Central School of Speech and Drama before training as a director, and has worked for the National Theatre, the Royal Shakespeare Company, Bristol Old Vic and the Chichester Festival Theatre. Other television appearances include the award-winning drama documentary "Joey" and three series of the late-night satire show "Who Dares Wins".

Richard Curtis is a scriptwriter best known for his work with Rowan Atkinson. He wrote sketches for "Not the Nine O'Clock News" and co-wrote all three series of "The Black Adder" and Rowan's two live London revues. In order to prepare for this book he studied Classics at Papplewick and Harrow School, and Greek at Oxford, under the patient care of the best teachers and in the company of the best friends he could have hoped for.

ODYSSEUS II
THE JOURNEY THROUGH HELL

Tony Robinson
and Richard Curtis

Illustrated by Tim Haws

BBC/KNIGHT

For my mum and dad, who got me educated proper, and for lovely Aoife and both her lovely legs.
Richard

For Mary, "sweet as the sight of land to the storm-tossed sailor."
Tony

Copyright © Tony Robinson and Richard Curtis 1987
Illustrations © Tim Haws 1987
First published in Great Britain in 1987 by the British Broadcasting Corporation/Knight Books

This book is based on the BBC TV series *Odysseus—The Greatest Hero of Them All* by Tony Robinson and Richard Curtis, told by Tony Robinson, produced by Angela Beeching and directed by David Bell.

British Library Cataloguing in Publication Data

Robinson, Tony
    Odysseus II: the journey through hell.
    I. Title   II. Curtis, Richard, *1956*–
    III. Haws, Tim
    823'.914[J]   PZ7

ISBN 0–340–42094–4
    [0–563–20617–9] BBC

Printed and bound in Great Britain for Hodder and Stoughton Paperbacks, a division of Hodder and Stoughton Ltd., Mill Road, Dunton Green, Sevenoaks, Kent. TN13 2YA.
(Editorial Office: 47 Bedford Square, London WC1B 3DP) by Cox & Wyman Ltd., Reading, Berkshire.

Contents

Prologue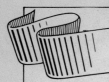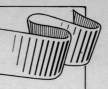

For ten long and terrible years the City of Troy lay under siege – the Trojans trapped inside, the Greeks camped outside unable to break in. People thought the war would never end. Then Odysseus, the Greatest Hero of all the Greeks, had an idea.

The Greeks sailed away, and left a giant horse outside the city gates as an offering to the Gods for their safe return to Greece. The Trojans couldn't believe their eyes. They dragged it into the city and threw a huge party. But it was the last time they would ever celebrate, because the whole thing was a trick. The Greek fleet had been hiding in the next bay; and the horse wasn't a gift – it was a trap. Fifty commandos were hidden inside it, and when night fell they crept out, opened the gates and gave a signal. The boats returned and the entire Greek army poured into the city ready for slaughter. By dawn Troy was burnt to the ground and its people were dead. It was a terrible end to a terrible war which, like all wars, had brought only suffering and more suffering.

Next day, as the Greeks sailed off, loaded with looted treasure, something stirred among the ashes of the blackened city. It was the White Goddess. She wasn't going to let the destruction of Troy go unrevenged, and she had something special planned for Odysseus – something very special indeed. As his boats sailed towards the horizon, their course set fair for home, he thought his troubles were behind him.

But they had hardly started. The journey home wasn't going to be easy. In fact – it was going to be A JOURNEY THROUGH HELL.

I

The Fat Batsman

Five Greeks, wearing nothing but shiny brass helmets, leapt off a big black rock and splashed into the waves. Further along the beach there was a game of cricket in progress, with three swords stuck in the sand for stumps; while out at sea some of the braver men were windsurfing on their shields. The whole bay was jam-packed full of Greek sailors on holiday, and they were all blissfully happy. All, that is, except Odysseus.

What was the matter with him? He wasn't sure himself. After all, the war was won, his ten ships were brim-full of Trojan treasure, and now there was even time for a few days rest and recreation on this beautiful tropical paradise before he set sail for home – home to the island of Ithaca, home to his wife and son. He ought to be feeling really pleased with himself. But there was something nagging at the back of his mind.

He stopped for a moment and smiled absent-mindedly at a sailor who was making sand pies in his helmet. Beyond was the jungle – huge, red and purple trees full of cockatoos, and insects the size of kingfishers.

And then he remembered his worry. He'd sent two scouts out at dawn to discover what food there was on the other side of the island. Where were they? They should have been back hours ago.

He frowned, drew his sword and began hacking a path into the jungle. Within minutes he'd found them. They were slumped under an enormous crimson tree, surrounded by piles of pink squashy fruit shaped like flabby rugby balls. Their bodies and hands were stained with juice and there were gobbets of fruit flesh all over their faces.

"You idiots," he sighed. "You've been eating that stuff again, haven't you? How many times do I have to tell you? DON'T MESS WITH LOTUS FRUIT – LOTUS FRUIT SCREWS YOU UP."

Four bloodshot eyes stared back at him. "Who are you, man?" mumbled one of the scouts vacantly.

"I'm your captain, idiot. Get back to your ship."

The scouts grinned – big dopey grins that meant nothing; but they didn't try to move.

"Are you coming?" asked Odysseus with a voice like thunder.

"Er, um, what did you say? . . . I was thinking about something else."

With a roar of frustration, Odysseus grabbed them by the ankles and dragged them back through the jungle.

Their heads bumped from side to side, bouncing against roots and tree stumps and boulders, but they never stopped grinning. Odysseus burst out of the trees and back on to the beach, and found himself face to face with more trouble.

The cricketers had started squabbling. An enormously fat batsman had been given l.b.w. but had refused to be out, and the fielders were throwing sand at him and calling him rude names.

"Stop that immediately," roared Odysseus, but the cricketers took no notice. He dropped the lotus-eaters and began to stride across the cricket pitch when . . .

"Odysheus! . . . Odysheus, shir!" Someone was calling his name in a very slurred voice. Staggering across the beach towards him was a scruffy, skinny, unshaven Greek sailor with a weaselly face. It was Thersites, and he smelt like a brewery. Today, life was nothing but trouble.

"You," said Odysseus, "are drunk."

"Me, shir. No, shir. Impossible, shir. There'sh no booze on the island, shir."

"But there is on board ship, isn't there Thersites? The sacred wine that *you* stole from the Trojan temple. Wine so strong that one swig of it and you're plastered for a fortnight. You've been knocking it back in secret, haven't you?"

"No shir. Absolutely not shir. Just one itsy-witsy

teeny-weeny drop, shir. I'm extremely sor . . ." but he never finished the sentence. His face turned green, his eyes crossed and he collapsed flat on his face.

Odysseus lifted up the drunk sailor's shirt. Tucked in the top of his trousers was a bulging goatskin full of wine. He strapped it to his own belt, picked up Thersites and threw him in the sea to sober up.

By now the cricket match had turned into a full-scale riot. The players had pulled out the stumps and were squaring up to each other, the surfers were racing across the sand to join in, and the lotus-eaters were wandering about amidst the mayhem giving out lotus fruit.

Odysseus stuck two fingers in his mouth and blew a long piercing whistle. The whole beach fell silent.

"That's *enough*," barked Odysseus. "Discipline has completely fallen apart. Get back to your ships. We're sailing for Ithaca straight away."

There was a low mumble of sulky discontent. Then Eurylochus, the first mate, stepped forward. He was a tall, gangly man with round glasses and a high-pitched voice. "We can't," he whined. "There's not enough food on board, and the only thing the crew have eaten for days is cockatoo and lotus fruit."

"In that case," replied Odysseus, "I'll take a rowing-boat and go and search for food. I'll be gone for forty-eight hours. In the meantime you're all confined to your ships." He took Thersites and the Fat Batsman and the ten worst troublemakers, and they rowed towards a tiny green dot on the horizon.

As they approached, Odysseus leant on his oars and gazed ahead of him. It looked pleasant enough. But then . . . looks can be deceptive, can't they?

Soon they could see that the island was covered in fluffy orange bushes. Then a bush moved and began skipping up the hillside. It wasn't a bush at all – it was a sheep. The whole island was covered in bright orange sheep!

"Meat!" cried the Fat Batsman and leapt off the boat waving his sword. Immediately the sheep began racing in all directions, desperate to avoid the sword-wielding maniac. Then a particularly tasty-looking ewe veered to one side, the Batsman followed and suddenly they both vanished – Fat Ewe and Fat Batsman nowhere to be seen.

Warily the rest of the Greeks crept forward when . . .

"Ooooooh!" There was a low, satisfied moan from somewhere deep in the hillside. They raced onwards and found themselves staring into a cave the size of a cathedral. It was dark and gloomy, lit only by a few greasy torches twenty metres up; and standing in the middle of it with his mouth wide open and eyes like saucers, was the Fat Batsman pointing at a beautiful sight.

Stacked against the back wall of the cave were mounds of meat: legs of lamb, breast of lamb, neck of lamb, shoulders of lamb – enough lamb to feed the entire Greek Army.

"Oooooh Oooooh Oooooh!" went the Fat Batsman again. "Sunday roast. I haven't had a Sunday roast for ten years."

Thirteen mouths began to water and thirteen stomachs made silly little noises.

"Find some firewood," ordered Odysseus, "and start cooking."

Immediately, his men scuttled off into the shadows and came back with some massive, strange-shaped pieces of wood which they threw on to a bonfire.

"Look at this bit," said Thersites. "It looks like an enormous pipe-rack, sir."

"Don't be ridiculous," replied Odysseus. "It would need pipes the size of rowing-boats."

"Look at this," shouted someone else, dragging in a hollow tree trunk with a wooden bowl on the end. "It's a pipe the size of a rowing-boat."

"That's not a pipe," scoffed Odysseus. "You'd need a mouth the size of an elephant to smoke that."

"Surprise! Surprise!" called the Fat Batsman, and staggered out of the darkness carrying a gigantic set of wooden false teeth.

"I think we'd better get out of here," murmured Odysseus . . .

But it was too late.

At that very moment, a shadow fell across the entrance and a voice boomed "In you go, my pretty ones."

A hundred bright orange sheep flooded into the cave and when the last was in, a creature the size of a lighthouse moved into the doorway. It was impossible to see what it was, because it was so vast it blocked out the light – but it smelt disgusting. Then it leant forward, wrapped two hairy hands around a massive boulder and slid it across the cave's entrance. The crew was trapped.

Slowly the thing turned round. It was shaped like a human, but like no human the world had ever seen. It was completely toothless, it had a knobbly nose with long hairs dangling from the nostrils, and in the centre of its forehead was one big, bloodshot eye – it was a Cyclops.

The Greeks fell to the floor in a gibbering, quivering heap; all except Odysseus. Even though his men were shrieking with terror, he stood his ground. He ignored the monster's hideously misshapen face, its stinking breath and its solitary sleep-encrusted eye. He just stared straight up at it, held out his hand and said, "Good evening. I hope you don't mind us dropping in unannounced."

"Not at all my little friends," replied the Cyclops with a shifty smile. "Where's your ship?"

"We rowed here from . . ." began Thersites, but stopped when Odysseus stood on his foot.

"We're shipwrecked," interrupted Odysseus. "Would you care to join us for a bite?"

"Don't mind if I do," answered the Cyclops, and with one hand he shoved the wooden dentures in his

mouth, while with the other he picked up the Fat Batsman, bit his head off and swallowed him.

Now their terror was total. They were trapped in the home of a giant cannibal, with no means of escape.

Thersites, white-faced and panicking, drew his sword. "No one eats a friend of mine and gets away with it," he cried, and rushed at the creature. But he didn't get far. Odysseus tripped him over, then dropped to the ground and hissed in his ear, "Are you crazy? If we kill that thing we'il be stuck here for ever. We'll never shift that boulder on our own. No, we'll wait patiently till morning and escape when he takes his sheep out."

So wait they did, while the Cyclops picked the sheep up one at a time, milked them, burped, yawned, then slumped down on the floor and fell fast asleep.

Next morning the monster opened his eye, stuffed two more of the crew in his mouth for breakfast, heaved the stone back and let the hundred orange sheep waddle out of the cave.

"Now!" whispered Odysseus, and the men sprinted towards the entrance.

Slowly, the Cyclops turned, chuckled and Phooooooow! He blew the Greeks back into the cave.

SLAM! BANG! FLAM! They smacked into the mounds of meat and crashed to the floor.

"Don't run away," drooled the Cyclops. "I like Greek food." Then he left the cave laughing and rolled the massive stone back across the entrance.

"What are we going to do?" blubbered the sailors, rushing up to Odysseus and clutching him round the feet.

"Quiet," ordered their captain shaking them off. "Let me think." And he threw his cloak over his head and thought.

An hour went by, two hours. The crew sat silently in a circle waiting for the solution. Three hours, three and a half, then . . .

"I've got it!" said Odysseus snapping his fingers. "Fetch me the giant's walking-stick."

In a dark corner was a gnarled oak tree which the Cyclops used for a coat stand, and hanging from the highest branch was a walking-stick as long as a flag pole. The crew made a human pyramid, Thersites scrambled to the top and heaved at the stick.

He wobbled, the pyramid tottered then crashed to the ground, and ZOOM! The stick went skidding across the floor and landed at Odysseus' feet.

"Now sharpen it to a point with your swords, then hide it. We're going to get this guy."

That evening the boulder rolled away from the entrance, the Cyclops and the orange sheep poured into the cave and CRUNCH! The boulder was rolled back again.

"What's for tea?" demanded the Cyclops, and playfully ran his hand over the shaking pile of sailors. "I fancy a nice kebab."

"Would you like a drink first?" asked Odysseus politely and produced Thersites' goatskin.

The giant snatched it.

"What's your name?" he asked gruffly.

"No Hwan," replied Odysseus.

"No Hwan?"

"Yes," said Odysseus innocently. "My father was Chinese."

"Well, thank you, No Hwan," said the Cyclops and swallowed the wine in one gulp. "As a reward, I'll eat you last of . . ."

But he never finished the sentence. His face turned green, his eye crossed and he collapsed flat on his face. The sacred wine had worked a treat.

"Quick!" barked Odysseus. "Where's the stick?"

They dug deep into a pile of sheep's droppings, pulled out their giant weapon and plunged it into the fire.

Then, when its tip was red-hot, they tiptoed over to the Cyclops with the stick under their arms and HISSSSS! They jammed it deep into his one huge eye.

"AAAAAAaaaaaaaaaaaaaaaagh!!!!!" screamed the Cyclops. It was a scream that would have woken up the dead, and it certainly woke up all the other Cyclops on the island, who put on their dressing-gowns and rushed over to the cave to see what was wrong.

"You OK?" they bellowed.

"I've been blinded!" came the answer.

"Who by?"

"No Hwan!"

"No one?" they replied. "Then what are you making such a fuss about?"

"Because No Hwan is here with me now!"

"Well that's all right then, isn't it?" shouted the other Cyclops. "You like being on your own. Stop making such a fuss. We want to get back to sleep," and they stomped off back to their caves.

For the rest of the night the sightless Cyclops blundered round the cave searching for the Greeks. But they hid behind table legs, in the Cyclops' boots, under his old socks, and he couldn't find them anywhere.

Finally, towards morning, the sheep started bleating. They were hungry, they hadn't been milked and they wanted fresh air.

At first the Cyclops ignored their plaintive cries but they grew more and more insistent. Finally the giant heaved the boulder to one side and squatted by the entrance. Then, as the sheep pushed past, he felt their backs to make sure the Greeks weren't trying to hitch a ride to freedom.

Odysseus watched smiling as one by one his men slipped past, hanging on to the underside of the sheep's bellies.

Finally, he was the only captive left. He grabbed hold of the last sheep, a rather nice-looking ewe with an orange fringe and long curly eyelashes, and clung on to her stomach as she waddled to the entrance. As she went past, the Cyclops bent down to rub her neck and the ewe gently licked the tip of his nose.

"You love your old master, don't you?" said the Cyclops.

'Ye-e-es, I ce-ertainly doooo," bleated Odysseus as the ewe waddled off down the hillside.

Soon he was back with his men. Then they threw the sheep over their shoulders, raced to the boat and began to row.

Back at the cave the Cyclops looked puzzled.

"Wait a minute," he thought. "Sheep can't speak. I've been tricked," and he groped his way angrily to the water's edge.

"Cyclops!" called Odysseus from the safety of his boat. "If you want to know who No Hwan really is, he's Odysseus, King of Ithaca, grandson of Autolycus the Sheep-Stealer. Thanks for the sheep."

In blind fury, the Cyclops tore a huge rock from the sand and hurled it towards the taunting voice of Odysseus. But it was no use. The rock fell short and made a huge wave which picked up the tiny rowing-boat and pushed it far away from the Cyclops – back across the sea to the waiting ships.

That night the Greeks had a barbecue to celebrate – roast lamb cooked on an open fire. But Eurylochus, the first mate, just turned up his nose and pushed his plate away.

"You could have brought back some mint sauce," he said.

Meanwhile the Cyclops stood at the water's edge in the moonlight bellowing "Mummy! Mummy! Mummy!"

Slowly, the whole surface of the ocean began to move; then a roaring noise filled the air, the waters parted and out of the sea rose a figure the size of a mountain. It was the White Goddess.

"My poor son," she said. "Who has blinded you?"

From over the water came the sound of raucous singing. The Cyclops pointed and a tear ran down his cheek. "Those sailors," he said.

"Then they shall die," the Goddess whispered softly.

"And what about their leader?" asked the Cyclops. "What will you do with Odysseus?"

The Goddess gave a slow, cold smile. "I've something very interesting in store for him," she said quietly and sank back below the waves.

2

The Wind and the Wallabies

Thersites squatted in the crow's nest, chewing peanuts. "How long before we get home?" he sighed. "We've been sailing for weeks now and there's still no sign of land; just wave after wave after . . ."

But suddenly he dropped his bag of nuts, which cascaded on to the heads of the crew below him. What was that tiny shining blob on the horizon? Was it a boat?

"Ship ahoy!" he shouted, and the lookouts on the other nine boats took up the cry. "Ship ahoy! Ship ahoy!"

The little blob was getting bigger now, and soon Thersites could see it wasn't a ship at all. It was shaped like an upside-down saucer, it was made of shining metal, and it was speeding towards him at a hundred miles an hour. It was an island – a huge man-made bronze island, and any second it would smash the fleet to pieces. The sailors shrieked and braced themselves for the impact when – WHOOSH! It opened like a book and the ships sailed right into the heart of the island itself.

Then GUDUNG! It slammed shut again and the Greeks found themselves bobbing up and down next to a bronze jetty in the middle of a little island harbour, surrounded on all sides by shiny walls.

At the end of the jetty was a huge building with two enormous sliding doors in its centre. The Greeks watched in fear as these slowly opened – what kind of monster had trapped them in this huge metal trap?

But it wasn't a monster at all. Instead, two tiny little bronze creatures with tiny little metal faces and pointy ears peeked around the side of the doors and then – scuttle! scuttle! – shot off down the corridor behind them.

"Get 'em!" yelled Eurylochus, and the Greeks burst off their ships and sprinted and slid down the shiny corridors in hot pursuit. Deeper and deeper they wound through corridor after corridor, until suddenly they emerged into a big echoing hall, which was full — not of weapons, or people, but of large bronze playthings. There were swings and slides and roundabouts and big-dippers; there were fruit-machines to put your money in and if you won, lemons and cherries and oranges poured out; there were "Test the Skill of the Charioteer" machines; machines in which tiny soldiers threw spears at tiny Thracian Invaders; and scampering in and out of these miraculous inventions, chattering away and clapping their hands, were dozens of the little bronze creatures in white coats.

"Can I have a go, sir? I wanna go!" screamed the sailors and searched their pockets for loose change. Then they jumped in the big-dipper cars, clambered on to the swings and crowded round the fruit-machines, jostling each other to put their money in.

Odysseus slowly shook his head from side to side. What a bunch of yobbos his men were! Then he felt a hand on his shoulder and a soft voice said: "You are Odysseus, the hero of the Trojan War. Follow me, I have something special for you."

Odysseus turned and found himself staring at a tall, upright, old man with long, grey hair down to his knees.

"I am King Aeolis, the inventor," he said. "This is my island, I built it. And these," he said pointing to the pixie-like creatures, "are my children. I built them too."

He took Odysseus to a tiny room, far away from the

noise of the machines, and gently handed him an ebony box covered in bulls' heads and double axes.

"This box is for you – the Greatest Hero of Them All," explained the King. "To get home, whisper the name of the wind you require, point the box towards your sails, open the lid to the width of one human hair, and it will blow you to your destination. But handle it with care. It took me twenty years to build it, and it is not without danger."

But when they returned to the hall, it was in chaos. His men had run out of money and were tilting the machines, smashing the glass, kicking in the panels of the roundabouts and teasing the King's bronze children by picking them up by their ears and dangling them over the top of the big-dipper.

"Back to your ships!" roared Odysseus. "We're going home."

With a whoop of glee the Greeks shot off down the corridor, leaving King Aeolis and his creatures knee-deep in broken machines.

Odysseus turned to Aeolis to apologize for the mess. But the wise old man didn't seem to care too much. "We can fix all this in a day or two," he said. "It's the box that took me years. Be careful with it."

Once they were on board, the island opened up, and Odysseus whispered into the box. Suddenly a warm south-west wind slapped the sails. They were on their way!

For five days they sailed and Odysseus never slept. He was nearly home now and he was determined that nothing would go wrong. He steered, he navigated, he hoisted the mainbrace – then, on the sixth morning, his eyelids began to droop.

"If I can only stay awake another hour," he thought. "Ithaca's just over the horizzzzz . . ." and as his island home came into view, his head slumped on to the ebony box.

Thersites was leaning over the side fishing for crabs. "'Aaah!" he went. "Look at sir, he's fallen asleep. He works so hard looking after us all, doesn't he?"

"Yes," replied Eurylochus, "and he's so popular. Think of all those lovely presents people give him."

Thersites frowned as he pulled a little crab out of the water, broke off its legs and stuck it in his mouth. "It's funny about the presents, isn't it? I mean, why does old sir always get them, and never us?"

"Exactly," snapped Eurylochus. "We're completely presentless, and yet there's old Mr Popular with more gifts than he knows what to do with." And their eyes slowly focused on the ebony box. "What do you think's in there – money, jewels . . . gold?"

The two sailors looked around to make sure that no one was watching, then quietly tiptoed over to their captain, lifted his arms, slipped out the box and flipped back the lid.

PHEEEEEOOOOW! A mushroom cloud of whirling wind shot into the air. The sails billowed and

ripped, the boat turned 180 degrees, and went hurtling back in the direction from which they'd come. Odysseus jerked awake just in time to see his beloved Ithaca disappearing from view. He cursed, he raged, he stamped, he shouted, but it was too late. Soon they were back at the island of Aeolis, but this time there was no warm welcome.

"I gave you my life's work," said the King bitterly, "and you wasted it. I wash my hands of you." And the little creatures uncovered a bronze bellows the size of a whale, and began pumping it up and down. Immediately a howling gale of biting, cold wind hit the Greeks and sent the ships spinning and speeding away from the bronze island once more – but not towards Ithaca. This time they were heading in the opposite direction, towards the frozen wastes of the far North.

It grew colder and colder till the decks froze and the men's beards turned to icicles and snapped off. On the third day, two icebergs covered in penguins loomed out of the mist and smashed together, crushing the leading boat. On the fifth day a giant blue squid wrapped its tentacles around the last boat and dragged it below. Then on the seventh day the whole sea froze over. Thick, green ice completely surrounded them, growing thicker and thicker by the minute until CRACK! CRACK! CRACK! Three more ships were crushed like walnuts in a nutcracker. And as their masts sank slowly beneath the ice, Odysseus thought he could see the face of the White Goddess way below on the bottom of the ocean – and she was winking at him.

He was afraid they were all doomed, but then, as quickly as it had come, the ice disappeared and, slowly at first but then faster and faster, the five remaining ships lurched forward, caught in an invisible current that dragged them towards the unknown.

But for once, when they got there, the unknown didn't look too bad. As the ships slowed down, the Greeks saw ahead of them a pretty little fiord, covered in snow and Christmas trees. The leading boats coasted in, and the men jumped out on to a stone harbour, slightly hysterical and very glad to be alive.

Only Odysseus' boat remained moored in the fiord. "Remember the Cyclops," he told Eurylochus. "We don't want more trouble." He cast his eyes across the surrounding hills. Everything did seem quiet enough.

The men on land soon came across a sweet little village, tucked into the side of a snow-capped hill. All the houses were made of wood and outside them were big, roasting pots. "They must be for cooking moose," joked one sailor, and certainly there was a slightly odd smell around, of a meat they didn't recognize. They headed on a bit further, and came to the town square. Round it were long wooden tables, covered in shallow soup bowls, as though a crowd of people had been having a meal.

"Must have been beetroot soup," another sailor observed, seeing as how the bowls were stained red. Then someone else found a bowl with a drop of soup left at the bottom and had a sip to see if his friend was right. But it had gone a bit hard and tasted foul. "Nope, it's certainly not beetroot," he said, then took a closer look at the bowl.

Only it wasn't a bowl at all. It was the top half of a skull!

Then he realized what he had just tasted. Blood!

Suddenly, from inside the wooden houses came a chorus of terrifying crackles.

"Cannibals!" yelled someone and the sailors began scrambling back to their boats. Charging across the square were hundreds of burly men and women with leather skirts, yellow plaits, metal helmets and massive knives and forks which they hurled at the Greeks, bringing them down in a hail of cutlery.

A few survivors reached the ships and began to pull out to sea, but now gigantic snowballs were tumbling down the hillside and smashing them to pieces.

The harbour turned red and the air was filled with the cries of dying sailors. Then there was silence, absolute silence, broken only by the sound of the occasional dead Greek being dragged up the hillside and plopped into a sizzling pot.

Only Odysseus' boat was safe. His sailors stared in frozen horror at the carnage. Then, "Row men, row!" yelled their captain.

Panic-stricken, they heaved on their oars. No one spoke, no one cried, every ounce of strength was devoted to getting away from the horror they had witnessed. They rowed till their muscles ached, their hands bled and their palms were covered in blisters the size of mushrooms. All that night they rowed, until the harbour, the fiord and the frozen North had been left far behind them. Then just before dawn, they saw the dark outline of an island. A little wave carried them up on to the beach and they flopped over the side on to the warm sand, and lay there starving, shivering and exhausted.

Odysseus' mind was reeling from what had happened. Nine hundred of his countrymen killed. Was he to blame, or was some unseen force still out to punish him for what had happened at Troy?

At that moment he sensed something looming out of the darkness. His old hunting instinct told him what to do. In a flash he had drawn his bow and THUMP! THUMP! THUMP! pumped three arrows into the shadowy creature. There was a whimper of pain, then the thing crashed on to the beach.

Thersites scampered over to see what it was. "It's a deer," he said sadly. "See its little face, it looks almost human . . ." but he drew his knife and began cutting it up, nevertheless.

"You are revolting," wailed Eurylochus. "How can

you eat flesh when you've seen your comrades squashed by a squid, battered by icebergs and chopped into tiny pieces by fork-wielding cannibals? I'm going to become a vegetarian!''

"Do what you like,'' replied Odysseus. "There's meat here for those who want it. If you don't, find something else. I'm too tired to argue.'' And he slumped down on the sand and fell fast asleep.

"Well, I'm going to search for fruit and nuts,'' said Eurylochus, and a dozen men went with him. They struck off into the forest which lay beyond the beach. Trees which were twisted into dark threatening shapes loomed out at them and scratched their faces. Bats whirled around their heads, and crackly insects dropped from the branches and buried themselves in their beards. But as dawn broke, they broke through the undergrowth and, to their amazement, saw ahead an elegant, white marble house surrounded by a smooth, sloping lawn dotted with statues. And from inside the house, lights blazed, music played and there was the sound of laughter.

They ducked behind a bush shaped like a peacock and watched. The smell of food wafted out of the house towards them – food that smelt so appetizing that their stomachs began to gurgle.

Then Eurylochus felt something tickling the back of his neck. He shrugged and wriggled, but whatever it was, it didn't go away. A cold feeling hit the pit of his stomach – it wasn't a spider, was it? . . . Or a poisonous scorpion waiting to strike? Slowly he moved his hand and reached round to feel his neck. His fingers touched something huge, warm and hairy. He turned in terror and found himself face to

face with an enormous lion.

He gave a tiny squeak of fear, slumped to the ground and FLOMP! The lion flopped on top of him.

"Help!" he moaned. "Help!" But his men couldn't save him. They were too busy looking after themselves.

From out of the darkness, their eyes sparkling with hunger and their fangs gleaming, a pack of tigers, jackals, bulls and rhinoceroses was coming towards them. Closer, and closer, and closer.

"I order you to help me!" cried Eurylochus, but by now the men were out of earshot, backing away in terror from the approaching hungry pack. "To the house, the house!" yelled a petrified sailor, and the others took his advice and charged in panic towards their only hope of safety.

"Let us in! Let us in!" they begged, hammering on the door. Slowly, it opened, the doorstep flooded with light and a deep, husky, woman's voice said "Hi boys, I'm Circe. Come on in."

Inside, the walls and floors were dazzling white with black furniture and enormous bright green pot-plants. All was peaceful. A python hung from the chandelier, there was a small dance-band made up of two baboons with flutes and a puppy on drums, and dancers shuffled round a dance floor – a goat and an ostrich dancing cheek to cheek, and a few wallabies doing a tango.

"Are you hungry?" asked Circe. She was tall and thin, with wild black hair, a black silk dress, bright red lipstick and a string of pearls.

"Mmmm!" the men nodded and Circe showed them to a black, polished table.

Immediately, out of the kitchen dashed a dozen chimpanzees with red bow ties and plates piled high with vegetarian food.

Now some people might have thought it puzzling to be served at table by monkeys; and most people would have found it strange to be entertained by a band of baboons. But these men were so hungry, and so relieved to be away from the wilder animals, that they just didn't notice – more's the pity.

They snatched the food from the waiters' hands and began cramming it in their mouths, rubbing it in their faces, and plunging their arms in it up to their elbows.

The band stopped, the dancers stopped, and Circe smiled.

It was an evil smile.

"You eat like pigs," she said. And then hissed, "Now become pigs."

But the men weren't listening. They just kept stuffing themselves with food. And at first they didn't notice that they were finding it more difficult to eat, and that their hands were hard and didn't seem to have any fingers any more. And then they did begin to notice – that their noses were suddenly longer, and that they kept slipping off their chairs. But when they tried to cry out to complain, it was too late. Instead of voices coming out of their big hairy mouths, they just snorted like pigs. Exactly like pigs.

Meanwhile Eurylochus' lion had fallen fast asleep.
The first mate wriggled out from underneath it and
crawled to the house. He peered through a window.
But where he expected to see his men, he saw pigs
scrambling over the floor. Filled with fear, he counted.
He had had twelve men. There were twelve pigs.

He raced back across the garden, through the wood
and down to the beach.

"Sir! Sir!" he cried. "Our men are pigs."

"They certainly are," replied Odysseus. "Let me
get back to sleep!"

But when Eurylochus explained what had
happened, Odysseus sprang into action. He bloomin'
well wasn't going to lose any more men today.

"Fetch a sword," he said, "then take me to the
White House."

38

"No way!" replied Eurylochus. "I'm getting off this island quick."

Odysseus looked at him with contempt, then turned and walked inland alone.

When he arrived at the house, he knocked on the door. Once again it swung slowly open. "Hi. I'm Circe. Come on in."

Odysseus followed the tall, dark woman and she sat him down at table and snapped her fingers. Immediately the twelve chimps appeared with plates of steaming food. Odysseus took a spoonful of curry.

"I like your snake," he said.

"Yes," replied Circe, "he's an old friend."

She glanced up at the python, and in a split second, Odysseus had flicked the curry in a plant-pot and his spoon was empty.

"A little more?" she asked. Odysseus shook his head.

Then suddenly the band stopped, the dancers stopped, and Circe smiled that evil smile.

"Very well," she hissed. "You eat like a gazelle. Become a gazelle."

But nothing happened.

"I said become a gazelle."

Again nothing.

Then a look of panic flashed across her eyes. "You didn't eat, did you?" she demanded.

"No," replied Odysseus, leaping across the table and drawing his sword. "Now die, witch!"

But Circe dropped to the ground and clutched Odysseus round the knees. "Spare me!" she begged. And the wallabies and the chimpanzees clutched him round the knees too, "Yes, spare her!" they implored.

"Why should I?" said Odysseus, the sword still at her throat.

"Because, because . . ." she stuttered, ". . . if I die, your men will be animals for ever. But if I live, I'll free them. And I'll give up being a witch, we'll have wine and feasting, the wallabies will entertain your men – and I'll give you your heart's desire."

"Do you swear it?"

"Yes – I swear it on the name of the White Goddess, the creator of all things, Protectress of all creatures." Slowly Odysseus edged his sword away from her throat.

"Now what is your heart's desire?"

Odysseus yawned. "A nice, big bed, please," he said. "I haven't had a proper sleep since we left Troy."

Days, weeks and months went by and the m
started getting restless. Finally they hammered on
Odysseus' bedroom door.

"Let us in!" they shouted. "You've been in that
room for a year and you haven't come out once."

"Why didn't you wake me up before?" grumbled
Odysseus, rubbing his eyes.

...ing? We were having fun with the

replied Odysseus, putting his boots
...ave overslept. Circe, how do we get
...ere?"
...ossible," she answered. "Too difficult, too
comp...d for any man."

"*That's* impossible!" shouted Odysseus, as his hope
of reaching home slipped away from him once again.
"Surely someone must know the way."

Circe gently kissed his forehead. "No. The only
person who can help you is the prophet Tiresias."

"But he's been dead for hundreds of years!"

"Exactly," said Circe, and unrolled a torn and
faded map. "If you want to get home, you must visit
THE LAND OF THE DEAD."

3
The Faces of the Dead

At the pace of a snail, the boat made its way up the
cold grey river, and once more Odysseus unfolded the
tattered map and stared at the writing.

"At the end of the ocean is a sea,

At the end of the sea is a river,

At the end of the river . . . is the Land of the Dead."

red,
ud
as its
river
n looked
, and then
orror.
Staring ⟨...⟩ at them
from above were a
hundred, huge, cruel
faces – gigantic carvings,
the remnants of some
ancient civilization.

"This is the place,"
announced Odysseus.
"This is the gateway to
the Land of the Dead."

The men began to
shudder and Eurylochus
rushed to his cabin and
barricaded the door. But
Odysseus just took his
sword, jumped over the
side, and headed for dry
land. He was past fear.
He knew what he had to
do, he had his
instructions and to hell
with the consequences.

He found himself in a stinking, boggy marshland.
Great clouds of mosquitoes rose out of the reeds and
swirled round his head, blinding and choking him.
But on and on he waded, with the map held high

above his head. When he g[...]
up on to the dusty shore, and loo[...]
was looking for a waterfall and a colum[...]
and the entrance to Hell.

*   *   *

It didn't take him long to find the waterfall. Just on
the other side of the hill it came crashing down,
spraying its water for hundreds of metres around.
Odysseus licked the spray off his arms, and knew for
sure he was in the right place. Its taste was salty. This
wasn't real water at all. It was a waterfall of tears. All
the tears the Dead had ever shed.

And just above the waterfall was the other thing he
was looking for. Bubbling out from beneath a huge
boulder was a thin stream of lava . . . molten fire.
Odysseus drew his huge sword, tensed his muscles
and WHAM! smashed the great boulder with one
blow. It splintered, and the stream of fire turned into
a torrent that poured down into the waterfall. The
moment the two met, a huge pillar of salmon pink
steam shot up into the air. Higher and higher it
rocketed, until its top had disappeared into the
clouds.

Odysseus threw his arms wide open.

"Spirits of the Dead," he called, "show
yourselves."

There was a clap of thunder, followed by a bolt of
lightning which wrapped itself around the column like
a snake around a tree. Then a face began to appear in
the steam. A grey, ghastly face with a big grin. It was
the Fat Batsman.

ice. "I bet you

st?"

ask the Prophet

e all day," continued the
n."

eath, then stepped into the
e was in the grip of a powerful,
hurled him up into the sky.

er he shot, spinning round and round
unt... ...G! He came to a standstill. He was in a
strange ...ld of multicoloured fog. Swirling, cloudy
shapes billowed all around him and the far off cries of
tortured souls echoed in his ears.

"It's hell in here," said a giggly voice by his side. It
was the Fat Batsman again. He'd always had a pretty
weak sense of humour, which death clearly hadn't
improved. Odysseus smiled grimly but politely, then
asked where he could find Tiresias.

"Go *that* way," replied the Fat Batsman pointing
through the swirling clouds. "You can't miss him."
Odysseus turned to leave.

"Oh! and send my love to the crew," he added.

"Yes," replied Odysseus. "Anything else?"

"No," said the Batsman. "Oh, yes, sorry, one thing
– you've only got one hour to find Tiresias. If you stay
any longer you'll die . . . horribly."

"Oh, great. Thanks for mentioning it," replied
Odysseus, and set off at speed.

After some time, he saw coming towards him an
old, ghostly woman with a dark veil over her face.
Odysseus rushed up to her. "Excuse me. Am I going
the right way for the Prophet Tiresias?"

At the sound of his voice, the woman dropped her veil. Odysseus couldn't believe his eyes. This was his worst dream come true.

"Mother," he gasped, and fell to his knees. "I didn't . . . I didn't even know you were dead."

His mother's grey, ghostly hand reached out and touched his head, then slowly her bony fingers began to comb his hair.

"Look at the state of you," she moaned. "Your hair's sticking up, your clothes are torn and there's a dirty mark on your face!" And she drew out a ghostly, grey handkerchief, spat on it and wiped his face.

"Go home, son," she continued. "Everything there's in such a state. I'm dead, the country's ruined and as for your wife Penelope . . ."

"Yes?" asked Odysseus anxiously.

"Well, she's in awful . . ." But before she could tell him, his mother's voice started to fade and her body began to disappear.

"Mother," he cried, "don't go! Talk to me! Talk to me! MOTHER!"

He flung his arms round her and tried to hug her, but there was nothing to hug – only a few wisps of grey cloud. In seconds she had completely vanished.

But he dared not stand and mourn her. Time was ticking by. He had only forty minutes left to find Tiresias. On and on he trudged and every moment the cries of anguish and despair grew louder. One man was begging desperately for a drink. He was tied to a stake, surrounded by a ring of blazing fire and just above his head was a bunch of succulent, juicy grapes. But every time he craned up to reach them, they rose tantalizingly out of reach.

Further on was a poor, lost soul pushing a mammoth boulder up a hill, only every time he got it within an inch of the summit, it slipped out of his hands and went careering back down to the bottom.

Then Odysseus saw something that in his heart he had feared since the moment he stepped into the Land of the Dead.

Ahead of him was a small, silent group of ashen-faced soldiers. They were wearing the uniform of the Greek expeditionary force and he recognized them instantly. They were his comrades from the Trojan War. He stared in sorrow at faces last seen lying dead on the battlefield – Achilles, Philoctetes, Patroclus – Great Heroes, all dead. And even more terrible, he saw comrades he had thought were still alive – his best friend Diomedes, Archbishop Calchas and, towering above them, still wearing his leopardskin head-dress, was General Agamemnon.

"How did you die?" whispered Odysseus. Silently Agamemnon held up his silver shield and Odysseus stared into it. It would tell the story.

Etched all around its rim was a scene Odysseus remembered only too well. It was the Greek port of Aulis, on that fateful day twelve years ago when the fleet had sailed for Troy. There on the hillside stood Agamemnon with a dagger held high above his head, about to kill his daughter; sacrificing her on a stone altar so that the Gods would give his ships fair winds. And in the background was his wife Clytemnestra, staring at her husband with hate in her eyes.

Then, the scene dissolved and the shield began to spin before Odysseus' eyes. New figures took shape – Agamemnon and his men camped outside the walls of

Troy, while back at home Clytemnestra plotted her revenge; with a new husband by her side, although Agamemnon was still alive.

And once more the scene changed. Now Agamemnon was returning home in triumph, his ships piled high with glittering treasure and weeping Trojan slaves. Odysseus stood hypnotized and watched as the General left his boat and led a triumphant procession from the harbour to the palace. The enormous double doors swung open and there stood his wife with a loving smile on her face. She beckoned her husband inside, he turned and waved to the crowd, climbed the long flight of steps up to the palace, and the doors swung shut.

The crowd seemed to hush. Then the whole shield erupted in agonized cries, followed by a long terrible silence.

BOOOM! The doors burst open again, and there stood Clytemnestra with triumph in her eyes and blood up to her elbows; with her new husband behind her, staggering under the weight of Agamemnon's body. He dropped it, and it rolled down the steps until it lay motionless in front of the crowd.

Odysseus shut his eyes in horror, and when he opened them again he was staring at a solid silver shield once more. Slowly he lifted his eyes and looked into the face of poor dead Agamemnon. The General's face showed no emotion, but a solitary tear trickled down his cheek.

It was more than Odysseus could bear. He gave Agamemnon a final salute, clasped the lifeless hands of his dead comrades, embraced the wispy form of his dear old friend, Diomedes, and then turned to go.

But at that moment he saw another figure, sitting far apart from the rest, staring into the distance.

It was Ajax, his old rival – Ajax who had hung himself when the Greeks had chosen Odysseus as their hero.

Odysseus walked across to the silent jug-eared giant, put one hand on his shoulder and held out the other in friendship. Surely he would forgive and forget now that he was beyond the grave? But no. Ajax's lip curled in contempt, and he turned and walked away.

Odysseus stared after him until he had disappeared into the mist. Then a pang of fear hit him at the base of his stomach. He had completely forgotten about the time, and now he had only five minutes to find Tiresias, or he would die himself and be trapped in this hell for ever. He turned desperately to his dead friends for help. They lifted their arms and pointed to a billowing bank of blue cloud. Odysseus sprinted towards it and burst through. He was shocked by what he found.

There, perched on a golden throne, was not the old prophet he had expected, but a tiny blind boy.

"Where is Tiresias?" Odysseus yelled, feeling death catching up with him every second. But the little boy just smiled.

"I am Tiresias," he said, in a childish tinkling voice, "ageless, out of time. I am Tiresias and you must listen to me very carefully, for your time is almost up. Your journey home will be full of terror, and you will only reach Ithaca safely if you follow my instructions carefully."

For five minutes Odysseus listened in terror to the fate that lay ahead for him. Such scenes of horror the boy described, that the King of Ithaca wept and shook his head in disbelief. If he had thought his sufferings were nearly over, he was wrong, so wrong.

"And finally," continued Tiresias, "when you reach your island home, you will discover an even worse horror. Your wife Penelope and your son Telemachus, whom you last saw in his cradle . . ."

"Time's up! Time's up! Time's up!" chorused a thousand twittering voices, and immediately the air was full of multi-coloured ghosts of all shapes and sizes, which wrapped themselves around Odysseus' feet, blew in his ears, and tangled themselves in his hair. They wanted him. They wanted to keep him. They wanted to keep him for ever.

Odysseus began to run. Faster and faster he fled until the billowing clouds ended and blackness began. He screwed up his eyes, dived into the black void and tumbled DOWN!
     DOWN!
     DOWN!

until . . . SPLAT! He landed in a wet sticky coldness which choked and blinded him. He lashed out wildly, struggling to the surface, desperately snatching for mouthfuls of cold fetid air. Where was he now – what nightmare was this? He opened his eyes expecting the worst, but . . .

No. It was the marsh! He had landed only a hundred metres from his ship! Slowly and agonizingly he crawled back to its safety, and once again the old stone carvings stared down at him. He had been through Hell, but they showed not the slightest interest – except for one. It was older than the rest, and so battered that it might have been merely a weather-beaten rock, but Odysseus knew that face – it was the White Goddess.

"Are you all right?" she asked. "Are you all right? Are you all right?" rang a persistent echo in his head. Only now he saw it wasn't the Goddess who was asking at all, it was Thersites shouting at him and shaking him roughly from side to side.

Then SPLASH! He'd been hit in the face by a shower of icy cold water, and there was Eurylochus standing over him with an empty bucket.

"Yes. I'm all right," replied Odysseus in a dazed voice. "And I've found out how to get home."

Slowly the ship sailed back down the river and, as his men swarmed across the decks and over the rigging, Odysseus watched them with a terrible sorrow. Tiresias had told him that every one of them would die before they reached home.

Should he tell them? No. "By the way, the Fat Batsman sends his love," was all he said.

When they arrived back at the ocean, it was completely still. There was no wind and there were no seabirds, just a lap, lap, lapping sound as the men rowed rhythmically through the water.

Then, on the third morning Odysseus held up his hand. "Listen!" he said. The men stopped rowing, and far, far away they heard a sound; a long low musical note, so quiveringly clear they were stunned by its beauty.

"What is it?" they asked in an awed whisper.

"It's the song the Sirens sing," replied their captain. "Soon we'll be passing their island," and he lifted a cask of beeswax from the bottom of the boat.

"If you hear the Sirens' song at full strength," he continued, "it will sound so incredibly sweet that you'll have an irresistible urge to join them on their island."

"Oh, good," Thersites chipped in. "I like a good singsong."

"You'd go straight to your death," snapped Odysseus, "like a thousand poor sailors before you. The ship would be wrecked on the razor-sharp rocks which surround their island, and the Sirens would drag you from the water and tear you to pieces."

The blood drained from Thersites' face. "Then what are we going to do?" he whimpered.

"Tiresias showed me the solution. I'm going to stuff your ears with so much wax you won't hear a thing," replied Odysseus.

When he had finished, he beckoned to Eurylochus. "First Mate," he ordered, "tie me to the mast."

"Pardon?" answered Eurylochus.

"Tie me to the mast," replied his captain.

"I can't hear you," said Eurylochus. "I've got wax in my ears."

Odysseus shook him until all the wax fell out again, then said, "No human has ever survived the Song of the Sirens. Tie me to the mast and however much I beg and plead, don't let me loose. Then we'll see what happens when a man hears their song . . . and lives."

So, tighter than tight, Eurylochus bound his master's hands and feet, and wound leather thongs round his legs and body and arms. Then he crammed a few fingerfuls of wax back in his ears, took up his oars again, and left his master to his fate.

As the hours went by, the magical sound grew louder. Odysseus was in ecstasy as first rhythms, then tunes and finally glorious harmonies made their way to him on the gentle breeze. Then the air was filled with singing – three exquisite voices. The words they sang were like words in a dream, and although they were in a strange, unknown language, yet he understood them completely. And whoever was singing, and whatever the words meant, Odysseus knew the song was just for him. And he knew that if he could only reach the singers he'd be happier than he'd ever been in his life.

Then the island itself came into view, but he didn't notice the murderous black reefs and the sandy beaches dotted with strange, white rocks. The song filled his head and pulsated through his body bringing tears to his eyes, and all he could see through the tears was a host of dazzling colours. To him the island was ablaze with a million exotic flowers, each one giving off a scent so intoxicating that his brain reeled. With a terrible cry he called to his men "Untie me! I order you! Untie me and let me live!"

He begged, he pleaded, he shouted, he threatened. He offered them his money, his palace, his kingdom, his wife, but the men were deaf; they just kept their heads down and rowed. Odysseus stared at the island in agony.

Suddenly there was a stirring among the flowers. Three flocks of goldfinches flew into the air and then the faces of three singing women appeared; the most beautiful women Odysseus had ever seen.

"Come to me. Come to me," they chanted.

He heaved and tugged at his bonds, but the harder he fought the deeper they bit into his skin. Soon his body was dripping with blood, his wrists and ankles were cut to the bone – but still he struggled.

Then a wave of fear hit him. The song was getting

softer. Soon he'd leave the beautiful women far behind. He cried out in a desperate panic, and the women rose from out of the flowers and began moving down the hillside towards the beach. Odysseus could now see that they weren't women at all, but huge, flightless kingfishers with fan-like tails and human faces. They were hideous, they were horrible, but still Odysseus was irresistibly drawn to them. If only he could bury his head in their soft, downy feathers, he'd be happy for ever.

But now the boat was pulling way, and as the song grew fainter, Odysseus' eyes began to clear and he saw the most terrible sight. What he'd thought were rocks weren't rocks at all, but the skeletons of shipwrecked sailors. The feathers fell from the Sirens

and then they weren't birds at all, but hideous fish-like creatures, slithering across the rocks, screaming at Odysseus to return. Soon they were perched on the peak of the highest reef, cursing and swearing, and tearing at their own skins in rage. They knew that if Odysseus didn't return they were doomed.

And he did not return. The boat was out of reach. In a final terrifying scream the voices of the monsters rose in hysterical fury and one after another they threw themselves off the pinnacle and smashed into the rocky sea below. Soon all that was left was a mass of sodden scales and fish bones like the mess in a fishmonger's slop-bucket. They were dead for ever. Odysseus had saved the world from the Sirens.

Not that he looked like a hero. He hung from the mast half-fainting, panting with exhaustion. But the spell was broken, and already it seemed nothing more than a ghastly nightmare. Gradually he became aware of a throbbing pain in his wrists and ankles. Then he heard Eurylochus' voice and opened his eyes.

"Are you all right?" asked the first mate.

"Yes. You can untie me now."

"Pardon," replied Eurylochus. "Sorry, I can't hear you."

4
Meat
(not a chapter for the faint-hearted)

Odysseus was feeling rather pleased with himself. "We did a good deed today," he said. "No one's ever going to get torn to pieces by those Sirens again."

He lay in the bottom of the boat and watched his crew cleaning out their ears. A gentle, warm breeze played across his face and a lonely albatross circled overhead while Eurylochus bandaged his aching wounds. In the quiet and the calm he thought to himself – "Perhaps Tiresias was wrong. Perhaps the agony is over. Perhaps we'll all be able to sail home in peace."

But Tiresias was not wrong. Odysseus and his men were heading for a hell on earth.

Suddenly the boat lurched forward and began to pick up speed. Thersites raced to the prow. Ahead of them was a long, black, jagged reef stretching from horizon to horizon. The surf crashed against it in deafening explosions, then fell back to reveal the shattered remnants of a hundred ships – torn sails, rotten masts, rotted bones. And Odysseus' boat was caught in a fierce current which drew it nearer to the deadly rocks every second.

"We're going to die!" screamed Thersites. "We're all going to die!"

But Odysseus could see a tiny gap in the rocks just

big enough for the boat to sail through. He grabbed the ship's wheel from the helmsman's clutches and steered towards it.

The men sprinted over to their captain and cheered and patted him on the back.

"We're not going to die!" screamed Thersites. "We're all not going to die! We're saved. We're saved."

But as the men kissed Odysseus' feet and stroked his beard in gratitude, his mind raced back to the words Tiresias had spoken. The blind boy prophet's tinkling voice rang in his ears saying: "Of all the hideous monsters in creation, the foulest and most terrifying are Scylla and Charybdis, and they live in the straits that pass through the long, black reef. In the cliff to the left lives the Dog Monster, Scylla. She has a long black tail, the body of a giant Dobermann Pinscher, and six vicious dogs' heads at the end of six long, snaking necks. When a boat passes, each head seeks out a sailor and chews him to pieces like a manky old slipper. On the right side lives the Frog Monster, Charybdis. He lies on the sea bed, opens his huge, froggy mouth, sucks the ocean into his bloated green body, swallows passing ships whole and then spits the bits out in a giant waterspout."

So, this wasn't going to be easy. Odysseus shivered as they sped into the straits, the cliffs on each side casting giant shadows across the boat. Then there was a deafening, sucking sound and the sea to their right opened up in a vast whirlpool – it was Charybdis, the Frog Monster.

At once, the men's cheers turned back to cries of terror.

"We're not saved after all!" screamed Thersites. "We *are* going to die!" and the men began racing around, grabbing their possessions and throwing the lifeboats into the water. But as they scrambled over the side, Odysseus grabbed each of them by the scruff of the neck and hurled them back on deck.

Before they could ask why, they understood.

The empty lifeboats picked up speed and hurtled towards the whirlpool. Once, twice, three times they sped round it, then down they plunged to their destruction.

From far below came a crunching sound. Then SPLUUUUME! The whirlpool turned inside out and became a giant, gushing spout of water, on the crest of which bobbed the remnants of the lifeboats, chewed to the size of matches.

"Hard to port!" yelled Odysseus. "Steer to the other side!"

Eurylochus raced to the prow and shouted orders as the boat veered hard over to the left-hand cliff.

"Keep your head down," ordered Odysseus.

"I know what I'm doing," snapped Eurylochus.

But he didn't.

He never heard the SNIFF! SNIFF! SNIFFING! from inside the cliff. He never saw the clouds of foul, dog's breath swirling above him, or the long, black neck snaking towards him.

But the crew did. They froze in horror as a dog's head the size of a killer whale came speeding down the cliff side.

Eurylochus stopped short, puzzled by the look on his comrades' faces. Then he turned to see what they were staring at. He didn't even have time to scream.

64

With one deft flick of her yellow tongue, a massive pink-eyed Dobermann had scooped him into her mouth, chewed him and swallowed him. Then her long neck shot back up the cliff, and in an instant she had completely disappeared. But from deep within the cliff came a THUMP! THUMP! THUMP! as her tail wagged from side to side in pleasure.

The sailors stayed rooted to the spot, paralysed by the loss of their first mate until, "DUCK!" barked their captain.

Five more jet-black necks were rocketing towards the ship, seeking their prey. Desperately the men tried to hide, but there was no escape. Through the rigging appeared one head; down the hatches sped another; through the cabins, into the wheel-house, below the decks, another and another and another. Until, with

five great barks, five dogs' heads retreated up the cliff with five pairs of legs dangling between their teeth.

There was no time for mourning; for at that instant the whole ship began to spin. It was heading back towards the whirlpool! Never had they been in a worse situation. Death to the left of them, death to the right and only the tiniest chance of survival in the middle. Odysseus looked to the left and heard the crunching of his sailors' bones, and then he looked deep down into the hideous dark spinning hole. Far below, he caught sight of Charybdis' wild eyes. Any moment they would disappear into the Frog's hungry green mouth. But at that final desperate moment, Odysseus felt a gust of wind and had an idea.

"Get your shirts off," he roared. "We need sails, sails, sails!" In an instant, a thousand buttons flew into the air as his men tore the shirts from their bodies and held them aloft.

On one side the whirlpool spun faster and faster, on the other the six dogs' heads began speeding down the cliff again. But . . . ninety-four shirts billowed, the boat shot forward and WHUMPH! it was out of the straits, and on to the other side of the ocean.

The crew shivered silently for a long time. Then some began to sob and moan. Soon they were clutching each other tight, holding on in fear and sorrow and homesickness. They might be safe, but sorrow was their only companion.

For days they drifted, not eating or speaking, until at last Thersites said "Cheer up. At least things can't get any worse."

But Odysseus remembered Tiresias' prophesy. "How wrong can you be?" he thought.

66

A week went by and the sea calmed, the sun rose, and there was the sound of bird song. There ahead of them was another island. But the crew didn't leap about in excitement; instead they asked themselves, will this place also be full of horrors? But as they got closer, their spirits rose. It certainly didn't look a dangerous place. There were fields of waving grass; cows dotted hither and thither like farmyard animals and it was completely uninhabited.

"It's perfect!" said the crew, as they sailed slowly along the coastline.

"Too perfect," replied Odysseus. "Sail on."

There was a groan of frustration and dismay but Odysseus went on, "We can't beach here. This is the island where the White Goddess keeps her cattle. Tiresias told me that if we kill even one cow we'll never get home alive."

"It's all right for you," protested Thersites. "You're strong and brave and good at games, but we're just ordinary sailors. We're fed up and frightened and exhausted. All we want to do is sit on dry land and eat our sandwiches. We won't touch her stupid cattle."

"Of course not," added the others. "I mean, some of us are even vegetarians. Please – let's stop and rest."

"OK," agreed Odysseus reluctantly. "But for five minutes, that's *all*." So they climbed off the boat, spread their table-cloths on the meadow grass and ate their sandwiches. In fact they were so well behaved, that Odysseus let them stay the night.

But when darkness fell, out of the sea appeared a dripping figure the size of a mountain. It was the White Goddess.

She reached up into the sky, pulled down a cloud, squeezed it and rain teemed down. She drew a deep breath, blew and there was a hurricane. She stirred the sea with her finger and massive breakers raced across the water. Then, having caused chaos, she smiled and slowly sank back beneath the ocean.

*　　　*　　　*

Odysseus woke with a start. "Storm!" he shouted. "Make the boat fast!" And knowing the ship was their only hope of survival, the crew leapt up, heaved it out of the water, lashed it down, and then climbed back on board to wait for the hurricane to end.

It was a long wait.

On the third day their sandwiches ran out.

On the fifth day their biscuits ran out.

On the seventh day their patience ran out.

Wrapping their clothes tight around them, they set off in search of food. The island was full of delicious-looking, chubby, brown cows, dripping with drizzle. They had big, soppy eyes and soft, round, pink noses. But the men were forbidden to touch them. Thersites looked at them wistfully and his mouth watered.

"I don't suppose . . ." he began, sharpening his knife.

"Leave those cattle alone," ordered Odysseus. "You're a vegetarian."

"All right. All right. I was only asking."

They combed the island for hours until they were soaked through to their vests and pants, but they found nothing to eat.

By the tenth day they were thin as rakes. "We'll be dead soon," thought Odysseus and took up his bow.

"I'm going to try again," he announced. "Who's coming with me?"

"Go on your own," replied Thersites, sulkily. "It's wet outside. We'll all get colds."

"All right," answered Odysseus, "but whatever you do, don't . . ."

"Yes, we know," chorused the men.

Odysseus left the boat, and the men smiled at each other. Thersites slipped out and shuffled off in the other direction. The men waited. There was a distant THUNK! Then Thersites returned.

"There's been a terrible accident," he said. "I was walking along with my sword over my shoulder, and I tripped over a cow, and accidentally its head fell off."

"What a shame," replied the men sympathetically.

"And now it's dead it seems a pity to waste it, doesn't it?" added Thersites.

"Oh, yes!" agreed the men, and went out to collect firewood.

Half an hour later, THUNK!, another sailor came back with another dead cow. "You'll never guess what," he said, "there's been a terrible accident . . ."

At dusk, a very wet Odysseus returned with berries and a dead rabbit. The smell of roast meat filled the air. All round the boat were shelters made of tarpaulin and brushwood, and underneath them were sailors sheltering from the rain, laughing, telling stories and singing "One man went to mow". Odysseus knew the terrible truth – his men were throwing a barbecue.

He strode up to them in fury.

"You swore you wouldn't kill the cattle," he raged.

"Don't worry," scoffed Thersites. "Stop nagging.

Sometimes you're just like my mother."

At that moment, a ghastly mooing filled the air. Everybody spun round. On Thersites' fire, a whole cow's carcass was roasting and the sound was coming from the dead beast's mouth. Then all the other carcasses joined in, all the chops and the steaks and the spare ribs and even the little hamburgers.

"Moo! Moo!" they went. "You're Doooomed! Doooooomed!"

Odysseus shivered. He knew what punishment was in store for his men, but he said nothing. Why spoil their last few hours on earth?

Next morning the wind had dropped, the rain had stopped and larks were singing in the meadows.

Thersites put his arm round Odysseus' shoulder. "You see," he said. "You were making a lot of fuss about nothing. Come on, let's get under way."

They dragged their boat back to the water and rowed off, with oars in one hand and cold chops in the other. Soon, the Island of the Cattle was out of sight, and they were all alone on an emerald sea, when . . .

CLICK!

The whole sky was plunged into darkness as though someone had switched off the light, and once again the dreadful mooing started. Soon it was so loud that the men slapped their hands over their ears in pain. Then, a single flash of green lightning illuminated the boat and the men watched in horror, as out of the sea, rose two white arms, a hundred metres from armpit to fingernail. Five massive fingers wrapped themselves around the prow of the boat, five massive fingers clasped the stern and . . . CRACK!

The ship snapped in two like a cream-cracker. Water gushed in and the two halves began to sink.

"Help us! Help us, Odysseus!" cried the men, but there was nothing he could do. They were miles from land and the lifeboats were lost.

Then, by the light of a second flash of lightning, Odysseus saw the deadly black fins of a school of sharks darting in and out of the wreckage. One after another his men, his faithful men – men of Ithaca he had fought beside and protected for over ten years – were pulled under the waves, kicking and screaming and doomed.

Only Thersites was left. His white face bobbed up and down as he swam towards Odysseus. Nearer and nearer he came. Odysseus stretched out his hand until their fingers were almost touching . . . But suddenly – YANK! Thersites shot backwards at a hundred miles per hour, with sheer terror on his face.

"Sir, sir!" he called in desperation. But it was no use, a split second later he disappeared; and where he had been, Odysseus saw only the giant fin of a shark and a little trail of blood.

Now six black fins veered towards Odysseus and began to encircle him – closer and closer with every circle. Soon they were so close he could see razor-sharp teeth and hear the hiss of fishy breath.

But Odysseus didn't die. A plump, white hand plucked him from the water, and as the sharks snapped round him, he was lifted high into the air. Two fingers and thumbs tied him neatly to a piece of mast and dropped him back into the sea, miles away from the sunken boat. Then, as suddenly as it had appeared, the hand was gone . . .

And Odysseus was completely alone.

All night long, he clung to that mast.

Then, as the first rays of light illuminated the sea, he heaved himself up to see where he was going. His heart sank. He was drifting back the way he had come – back towards the black reef and the twin monsters, Scylla and Charybdis.

He thought back to the terrible moment when Scylla had chewed up his First Mate, and realized it would be suicide to sail through the straits on her side. He would have to brave Charybdis, the Frog Monster.

Nearer and nearer he drifted, until, just as he entered the straits, he began to paddle desperately over to Charybdis' side. But there was nothing he could do. Once again there was a deafening, sucking sound, as though the plug had been pulled out of the biggest bath in the world, and the deadly whirlpool opened up in front of him. Around the edge of it he span, like soap in the plug hole. Any moment now, he'd topple into Charybdis' ravenous throat, to be chewed up and spat out like a grape pip. Then he glanced up and saw above him, growing out of the side of the cliff, a tiny fig tree. And he had an idea. That fig tree was his only hope – his life depended on a twig.

With all the strength he could muster he stretched up, snatched at an overhanging branch and held on tight.

The mast dropped from between his legs and plunged down the centre of the whirlpool to the ocean floor. Then, BLAM! the whirlpool became a water-spout as the frustrated Frog expelled two cubic miles of ocean from its swollen cheeks.

That was Odysseus' chance. With a desperate leap and split-second timing, he jumped and caught hold of the rocketing mast, gripping it with his arms and his thighs. VOOM! it shot upwards; SPLASH! it fell down into the sea; and ZOOM!, as he paddled like fury, it shot out of the straits and floated into the ocean on the other side.

He was safe. Totally lost, totally alone but at least he was alive. Then he noticed something soggy in his hand. It was a fig – a ripe, juicy fig. He bit deep into the luscious fruit until the juice trickled down his cheeks.

"Maybe," he thought, "just maybe, things will take a turn for the better now."

For nine days he drifted. His legs and toes began to wrinkle like a man who's fallen asleep in the bath. On the tenth morning he came to the island of Ogygia. He lay in the shallow water, too exhausted to drag himself up on to the beach, and looked up. Standing over him was the most stunning-looking young woman he'd ever seen. She'd shaved the sides of her head and coloured the central piece of hair red, green and aquamarine. From her ears hung huge, pearl earrings and on her shoulder cooed a yellow bird.

"I'm the nymph, Calypso," she said, pulling him to his feet. "I'm glad you've come to stay."

"I haven't!" replied Odysseus. "I'm the King of Ithaca, and I've got to get back to my wife and my son and my kingdom."

"A few more weeks won't make any difference," squawked the yellow bird.

Odysseus thought about it. He looked at the little grass hut, at the palm trees full of bananas and coconuts, at Calypso's beautiful, lonely face.

"OK," he said. "I'll just come in for a quick coffee."

5
Hero in a Frock

It was the longest cup of coffee ever. The days turned into weeks, the months turned into years, and still Odysseus stayed. And then one morning, sitting in the shade of a coconut tree, with a glass of rum in his hand, Odysseus plucked yet another grey hair from his beard and felt ashamed. He missed his son; he hadn't seen him since he was a baby. He missed his wife; he knew in his bones that she was in some kind of trouble. Why wasn't he back in Ithaca helping her? A lonely tear began to trickle down his face. The great hero had become a beach bum.

"He wants to go home," squawked the parrot. Calypso nodded, and there was a tear in her eye too. She knew it was true.

Sadly and silently she took Odysseus by the hand, led him into the forest and handed him a silver axe. Together they felled seven pine trees, lashed them together, stitched a sail, and then dragged their newly made raft down to the water's edge.

"That'll sink! That'll sink!" chirruped the bird.

"Don't worry, he's protected," Calypso replied.

"Protected!" scoffed Odysseus. "A thousand men left Troy, now there's only me!"

"And why do you think you're still alive?" asked Calypso, looking deep into his grey-blue eyes. "Someone's saving you for the greatest task of all."

Odysseus held Calypso tightly, then he pushed the

raft out to sea and jumped on board. The nymph and the parrot waved until he was a tiny dot on the horizon, and long after he had disappeared they stayed standing on the shore, sad and silent. Waiting for the next lonely sailor.

Meanwhile, Odysseus dangled his feet in the water and smiled as the fish nibbled his toes. Then, as evening came, he saw the Island of the Pirate King.

"Soon I'll be home," he thought to himself.

But, of course, life's not that easy. The parrot was right, the raft wasn't going to make it. At that moment, behind Odysseus the huge White Goddess rose out of the water like a huge white whale and blew him a lethal kiss. Well, not quite lethal, but pretty deadly.

The kiss became a ripple, the ripple became a wave, the wave became a tidal wave, and the tidal wave became a whole series of two hundred metre-high waves bearing down on him at incredible speed. He was hurled back and forth as his raft plunged up and down with sickening fury. "This is it," he thought. "I'm going to die now."

Then, out of the water leapt the most extraordinary sight he'd ever seen – and he'd seen a few extraordinary sights in his time.

It was a mermaid – a real live mermaid – looking just like he'd always imagined a mermaid would look; with long blonde hair, a fish's tail and a polka-dot scarf around her neck.

"Take your clothes off," she said in a fishy kind of way.

"Pardon?" replied Odysseus, lying flat on his stomach and gripping the edge of the raft.

"Strip off and jump into the water," she insisted. "This'll stop you sinking." And she wrapped her polka-dot scarf around his wrist, flipped her tail, and with a beautiful, curving dive disappeared into the ocean.

Odysseus looked up at the massive waves the size of mountains, then down into the inky depths of the raging sea.

"No way," he thought. "I'm staying put." It really didn't seem quite the moment for a striptease.

Then . . . CRACK! The raft split in two. He held on even tighter.

CRACK! CRACK! CRACK! Now all he had left to cling to was half a pine tree.

"Oh well, here goes," he murmured, wriggling out of his clothes and rolling into the water, with nothing but a scarf to his name.

And it worked. Gigantic breakers were crashing all around him, but with the mermaid's scarf around his wrist, he could do the crawl, the breaststroke, even the backstroke and never once did his head go under.

As the rocky outline of the Pirate Island came into view, he untied the scarf, spread it between his feet, took the next big wave, and surfed towards land. Up the river estuary he shot, then grabbed the branch of an overhanging tree and swung ashore with the scarf between his toes. Then he screwed the scarf up into a ball and hurled it back in the water.

A hand shot up and grabbed it, a fishy tail gave a wave of farewell and the mermaid swam off back to deep water.

"Pity," thought Odysseus. "I'd like to have got acquainted." Then he lay down behind a bush, covered himself with leaves and fell fast asleep.

*   *   *

Up at the palace, the Royal Family were asleep too. The Pirate King was snoring peacefully, tucked up in a bed made out of a lifeboat. Next to him lay the Pirate Queen, with a pipe between her toothless gums and a bottle of gin by her side. And in a room at the very top of the palace, Princess Nausicaa lay dreaming.

In her dream, her bedroom was covered in dirty linen, which she picked up and carried over to the laundry basket. But as she lifted the lid, a voice inside said "Surprise! Surprise!"

With a start, she woke up, raced over to her four handmaidens and shook them awake. Their dozy faces looked up at her blankly as she described her dream.

"What does it mean?" she asked.

"That it's time you did some washing?" they suggested.

Nausicaa let out an annoyed little shout. "Oo!" she went. Sometimes her handmaidens were too stupid for words. Nevertheless, on this occasion, they might be right. She'd been wearing the same pair of socks for a week, and her lovely white dress was now quite a few, rather unattractive shades of brown. Yup, it was time for action.

She sped down to her parents' bedroom, threw open the door (which was made out of a raft) and peering through the stale pipe smoke shouted, "Mother, may I borrow the ox-cart and go and do my washing?"

"Certainly, my dear," groaned a muffled hungover voice from underneath the blankets. "You can do mine an' all."

So the handmaidens loaded the cart with brown socks and brownish shirts and browny skirts and they all trundled down to the river.

"We should be finished by noon," announced Nausicaa cheerily.

But noon came and went and the dirty sock pile was still the size of a large rhododendron bush. The handmaidens were useless. They couldn't do anything by themselves.

"Miss! Miss! Miss! Which bit of the stream shall we wash the woollies in?" they chorused. "Miss! Miss! Miss! Shall we wring out the loin-cloths or just bash them with a big stone?"

Finally Nausicaa lost patience. "Forget it," she said sharply. "We'll sunbathe instead."

"Oh, no," moaned the handmaidens. "Our skin's too delicate. We'll come out in blisters."

"All right, we'll play ball then," snapped Nausicaa. "Honestly, what a lot of drips you are!"

And sure enough, the handmaidens were even worse at ball than they were at washing. They couldn't throw straight and their catching was pathetic.

Eventually, in frustration, Nausicaa hurled the ball so hard it hit a handmaiden, bounced off her head, and landed in the river.

The four handmaidens rushed to the water's edge in a dither and started shouting. "Help!" they went. "It's in the river. Quick! It's floating away. Oh, no, if it gets lost we'll cry and cry and cry."

Underneath his leaves, Odysseus heard the noise. What was up? It sounded like someone was in trouble. In a flash, he'd dived into the water and powered his way across to the thing bobbing up and down ahead of him. He grabbed it, turned and swam towards the shore. Was it a puppy? A kitten? A baby?

It was only as he clambered on to the river bank that the truth dawned on him. It was just a ball; a big, red, bouncy ball.

He snorted with amazement, then held it out to the four open-mouthed girls lined up in front of him.

They squawked, they giggled, they blushed scarlet, then they ran away and hid behind a tree.

But Nausicaa, Princess Nausicaa stood her ground.

"What was the matter with *them*?" asked Odysseus.

"You've got no clothes on," explained the Princess.

"Oh, yes. Sorry," said Odysseus and politely placed the ball in front of him. "I'm shipwrecked, I've lost everything."

"So I see," replied Nausicaa. "I'd better give you something to put on. My clothes won't fit you; try my mother's."

Later that day, Nausicaa, her handmaidens, and a rather large woman in a floppy hat and paisley frock entered the Pirate city.

It certainly was extraordinary. Everything in it was

to do with pirates. The houses had sails and the street lamps were made out of oars. Nearly everyone that passed had a parrot on his shoulder and a wooden leg. Some had two wooden legs. In fact some had two parrots and some of the parrots had wooden legs themselves. All the shops were full of eyepatches and hooks and cutlasses of every shape and size, labelled "Small and Vicious", "Medium and Fatal" or "Big and Good For Chopping Off Heads". Odysseus had never seen such a collection of people – dusky pirates with rings through their ears and scars on their noses, and skinny pirates with rings through their noses and scars where their ears had once been. And every one of these mean individuals just stopped for a second to take a suspicious look, with their one good eye, at the huge woman in the floppy hat and the paisley frock.

"Our pirates hate strangers," whispered Nausicaa. "If they knew you were a man they'd kill you. But you'll be safe in mother's clothes." Odysseus pulled his hat firmly over his face. He could handle a couple of pirates with his eyes closed. A shipful he could probably cope with on a good night – but a whole island's worth – nope, he'd rather wear a frock any day.

So he kept his head down, and finally he and Nausicaa reached the palace, parked the ox-cart and then made their way inside, picking their way down long, dark passages crammed with chests full of dusty treasure maps. Then they entered the smoky banqueting hall. A whale was roasting on an open fire, musicians were singing sea-shanties, two drunken pirates were dancing a hornpipe on the table, while a hundred hairy fists kept time.

Nausicaa and the big lady elbowed their way through the throng until they came to the high table.

"Noble King," said Odysseus in a squeaky voice. "I am Tinnia, daughter of Sciatica, a noblewoman from Ithaca. The ship in which I was travelling was wrecked in last night's storm. Will you help me return to my native land?"

The King smiled at the buxom damsel in distress standing in front of him, then lifted his eyepatch and winked at her roguishly.

"Certainly, Ma'am," he replied. "I've a boat leaving on the morrow. She sails right past Ithaca. Now sit down and eat."

Odysseus politely nodded his thanks and took his place. He couldn't believe his luck. At last he was going home.

86

Not that there weren't a few little irritations in store. A burly sailor, with five chins and a bulging belly hanging over his belt, waddled up to the Ithacan noblewoman and put a friendly arm around her shoulder.

"'Ullo darling," he purred. "You feeling lonely?"

"Go away," she hissed.

But the sailor didn't go away. Instead he pinched her on the cheek. Then he patted her bottom.

He soon wished he hadn't. The woman looked round to make sure no one was looking, then PHUMPH! She jammed her elbow into the flabby pirate's stomach. The pirate's mouth opened in surprise, but no sound came out. Then he slowly collapsed in a heap on the floor.

The Pirate King was too drunk to notice, but the Pirate Queen was not so inattentive. She puffed at her pipe and stared hard at the woman in the hat and the paisley frock.

*   *   *

Next morning Odysseus was sitting restlessly in the courtyard waiting to be off, idly watching some bearded buccaneers sorting through a pile of old treasure.

"How do you fancy feeling my muscles, darling?" asked a voice. Odysseus turned and saw it was the pirate with the five chins. He was clearly a man who couldn't take a hint, and now, with a dumb smile over his ugly mug, he rolled up his sleeves, flexed his biceps, picked up a great silver plate, threw it two hundred metres in the air, then ducked out of the way as it smashed down into the ground.

"Don't listen to him, I'm your man," roared a huge buffalo of a pirate with a jet-black beard and even blacker teeth, and he picked up a massive golden plate, hurled it three hundred metres in the air, caught it and dropped it in Odysseus' lap.

"Feel that," he said proudly. "It's a real whopper."

Odysseus fluttered his eyelashes. "Oh, you boys," he cooed. "You're so strong!" and so saying he flicked his wrïst, and the plate went soaring up in the air, over the palace roof and out of sight. There was a long silence, followed by a tiny splash as it fell into the harbour half a mile away.

The pirates stared in amazement. Never before had they come across a woman who could chuck treasure ten times further than they could.

"Now leave me alone," squeaked Odysseus. "Otherwise there might be a teensy bit of trouble." If there was one thing he couldn't stand it was show-offs.

The Pirate Queen stepped out of the shadows, still puffing at her pipe.

"You certainly pack a punch, dearie," she said.
"Come and have some lunch."

Inside the banqueting-hall was another roasted
whale, more drunken dancing and a troupe of pirates
on stilts, juggling with pieces of eight.

The King sat on his throne, chewing on a whale
bone and hammering the high table with a beer mug.

"Bring on the storyteller!" he roared.

"Yes! Yes! The storyteller!" echoed the diners, and
on to the high table leapt a small pirate with a
pointed nose and a striped T-shirt.

"I'm going to tell you a story," he yelled above the
hubbub, "about the Trojan War and those two
arch-rivals, Odysseus and Ajax."

"Hurrah!" went the pirates, then "Shssh! Shssh!
Shssh! It's the story of Odysseus – the Greatest Hero
of Them All." Immediately the hall fell silent.

"This was the ninth year of the War, OK, and the
Greeks were really cheesed off. So old Agamemnon
says, 'Right lads, we're going to have some games.
There'll be chariot racing, sack racing, egg 'n' spoon,
but the biggest prize, for the Champion of
Champions, will be the running race.'

So, they built this massive stadium with a marble
altar in the middle and a running track around the
edge, and the day of the games arrived and inside the
stadium it was chaos. There were spectators,
peanut-sellers, athletes with flags, cows wandering
round waiting to be sacrificed, priests wandering
round looking for the cows *to* sacrifice and one or two
cunning devils selling cut-price sacrificial swords.

The day wore on. King Menelaus won the egg 'n'
spoon, Diomedes won the sack race, Philoctetes and

Achilles won the three-legged. Then 'Quiet please,' roared Agamemnon. 'We now come to the highlight of the day's events. For a prize of a thousand gold pieces and a fortnight's holiday for two on Mykonos – the running race.'

The six finalists stood behind their marks. They were the six greatest heroes in the Greek army – Menelaus, Achilles, Patroclus, Ajax, Diomedes and last, but by no means least, Odysseus.

'On your marks – Get set – Go!' barked the Judge, and they were off! Straight away Menelaus sprinted into the lead, and by the end of the first lap, there was a gap of fifteen metres between him and the next man. Slowly but surely others pulled him back, until by the end of the second lap it was level-pegging again.

But the blistering early pace had taken its toll. Patroclus just couldn't hang on in there, and the others surged ahead. And had the pace-making taken it out of Menelaus? It certainly had – lap three and he limped off the track and slung in his towel. And could that be Achilles? Yes, Achilles had gone too – a recurrence of that old tendon trouble which could leave him on the sidelines for the rest of the season.

Lap four, and it was a three man race: Odysseus, Diomedes and Ajax. But then Ajax effortlessly moved up a gear, Diomedes couldn't stay with him and at the bell it was Ajax and Odysseus – Odysseus and Ajax, neck and neck. Then Ajax started to kick. He lifted his legs like a gazelle. Ten metres, fifteen, twenty – the gap between them was widening at every stride. Half way down the back straight Ajax was thirty metres in the lead; nothing could stop him now. The Big Man with the Big Ears was on his way to another record-breaking victory.

But Odysseus had never been beaten yet, and he certainly didn't want to start now. He looked up into the sky and yelled to the heavens 'Goddess, if you love cheaters and tricksters, if you love the man who wins by his brains and not by his brawn, help me now!'

At first, nothing happened. But then, as if by magic, one of the sacrificial cows lumbered on to the track, emptied its bowels, then wandered back on to the grass again.

Ajax came speeding around the final bend. He didn't notice the cow or the steaming brown pyramid in his path. He was too busy dreaming of the cheering crowd and the victory laurel-wreath resting on his head. He turned, sneered, and waved contemptuously at Odysseus.

SLURP! His foot hit the dung.

SWISH! His legs shot up in the air.

ZOOM! He skidded along on his stomach.

And DONG! His jaw hit solid earth and he lay unconscious on the ground five metres away from the finishing line.

Meanwhile, Odysseus politely dodged the welcoming cow pat, raced round his rival, and crossed the finishing line first. What a man! And that was how Odysseus, the Greatest Hero of Them All, won himself the prize of a fortnight's holiday on Mykonos."

"Hurrah!" yelled the Pirates again – they loved that story. They couldn't hear it enough times and, as the storyteller bowed, took his gold doubloon from the King and disappeared back into the crowd, all of them were doubled up with laughter. All of them except Odysseus. He'd laughed when it had happened, of course – split his sides at poor old browned-off Ajax. But not now. To him the men in the story were not just men in a story, heroes in a tale – they were real people, real friends. And now they were dead. The Trojan War hadn't brought them glory – it had brought nothing but misery and death. Softly he began to cry.

"Quiet, you dogs," hissed the Pirate Queen. "There's a spy in our midst; a stranger who is not what she seems. Tinnia, the Ithacan noblewoman who can throw a discus further than a pirate, who weeps at tales of the Trojan War, who is wearing *my* hat and *my* paisley frock – seize her!"

And in an instant, all the pirates snarled, picked up their cutlasses, snapped on their wooden legs and charged at Odysseus. In a flash, he brushed away his tears, drew his sword and leapt on the table. Then he flung off his floppy hat, tore off his frock and roared in a voice they felt they knew . . .

"Yes, I am an imposter. I am Odysseus, King of Ithaca, and I shall die as I have lived – by the sword!"

"Odysseus!" hissed the Pirate Queen.

"Odysseus!" murmured the awed pirates.

"Odysseus!" roared the Pirate King. "Grandson of my old friend Autolycus the Sheep Stealer! Odysseus who killed the Cyclops! Odysseus of the Wooden Horse! Odysseus, the Greatest Trickster of Them All! Welcome!"

Then the pirates cheered, the Queen gave him a sloppy kiss and they all listened spellbound for hours as the greatest trickster in the world told them the story of his travels.

At last evening came, and a thousand jolly pirates carried him down to the waiting ship. The Queen Pirate gave him a final hug and a fresh set of clothes, and the King Pirate, with great ceremony, handed him the Wooden Leg of Honour, the highest compliment a pirate can ever receive, as well as the Freedom of the Waves – freedom to loot every ship he ever came across.

Then with a roar from a thousand toothless pirate mouths, the Jolly Roger was raised and the Pirate ship set off for Ithaca. As it pulled away, Odysseus hurled something at Princess Nausicaa.

"Keep this to remember me by," he shouted.

Nausicaa burst out laughing. It was a ball, a big, red, bouncy ball.

Soon Odysseus' head began to nod. Past islands full of dragons they sailed, past gorgons, centaurs,

griffins and harpies. The sky turned green, yellow, red, indigo, pink, and finally a clear bright blue, full of fluffy clouds.

For twenty years he'd been away, and at last, ahead, were the low hills of Ithaca. But Odysseus didn't see them. He was fast asleep. And when they landed, the pirates gently lifted him off the ship, laid him down at the water's edge and sailed away.

Odysseus lay gently snoring.

He was home.

And it was a good thing he was getting plenty of rest. He was going to need it.

6
Beggar in the Rubbish Heap

Odysseus woke in a panic. His legs were shaking and he was drenched in sweat. Where was he? How had he got there? He crawled forward and peered over the edge, but immediately pulled back in shock. He wasn't on the ground at all, but hundreds of metres up in the air. He reached out to steady himself, but suddenly he realized something even more terrible. It wasn't cold hard rock that he was clinging to. It was something warm and throbbing: a huge white pulsating mass, carrying him up, up, away from the earth.

The awful truth suddenly dawned on him. It was a hand – the hand of some enormous creature and it was lifting him higher by the second.

He looked up and *then* all was explained. Gazing back at him was an expressionless face so big that it filled the entire sky – it was the face of the White Goddess.

Then her giant lips began to move and her voice reverberated around his brain.

"Odysseus, grandson of Autolycus the Sheep Stealer, I have protected you for one last heroic task. You are dreaming now, but when you awake take care, for this is what you must do." Then she lifted him up towards her lips, that were the size of two pink canoes, and she whispered her instructions in his ear.

And for the second time, Odysseus woke in a panic. But this time he was back in the real world. He shuddered with horror – what a terrible dream that had been. Could the tale the White Goddess had told him be true? He looked around to consult the pirates, but once again things were weird. What was he doing lying on the sand with his feet in a rock-pool? He should be on deck.

"Oh no! I've been stranded," he groaned. "They were meant to take me home, but instead the pirates have dumped me on another God-forsaken island. What's in store for me this time then – killer hippopotamuses? Twenty-headed giraffes? Giants with three noses who turn people into animals and then eat them with tomato sauce?"

He stood up, shook the water from his boots and surveyed the scene . . . He was ready for the worst.

But, surprisingly things seemed all right. In fact he rather liked the look of the place. There was a little rock, shaped like a mermaid, just like the one off which he'd learnt to dive when he was a boy. And there in front of him were fields just like the ones where he had learnt to plough. And behind them, were woods which reminded him of the woods where he had fought the wild boar and almost died. In fact, the whole place was suspiciously like . . .

Suddenly he gasped. For a full ten seconds he couldn't breathe. Two tears trickled down his cheeks, because now he knew the truth and felt it in every bone in his body. He was home.

At last he was back; twenty years on he was back in Ithaca, his home, his kingdom. This was the land where he would live out the rest of this life in peace.

Or so he thought.

He looked inland. Far away he could see a town, and overlooking it he could just make out the outline of a palace – his palace.

*   *   *

A jug of wine hurtled through the air and smashed against the shields and javelins lining the wall of the palace banqueting hall. There was a roar of laughter as red wine dripped on to the floor, staining it the colour of blood.

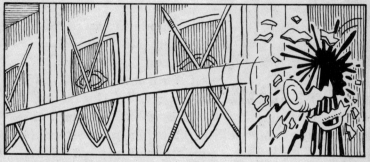

"Clear up that mess, Telemachus!" someone shouted.

"Do it yourself," replied a young man whose face was flushed with anger. He started to stride out of the room, but a leg shot out and sent him sprawling. There was jeering and cheering and a hundred drunken men chucked bread rolls in his direction.

There were two people, however, who didn't cheer, who didn't jeer. The first was an old nurse, dressed in black, who sat silently sewing. The second was Penelope herself, Odysseus' Queen. Her head was bowed over a half finished tapestry, and her eyes . . . were full of hate.

For ten long years these drunken louts had occupied her palace. And every day they said the same thing – "Face the facts. The war finished years ago. Your husband's dead. Marry one of us instead."

And every day for ten years, Penelope had replied, "I'm not strong enough to force you to leave my house, but I won't marry you."

But last month had been the 21st birthday of her son, Telemachus, and everyone in Ithaca knew the promise Penelope had made her husband on the fateful day he left for Troy. She had promised him – **If he hadn't returned by the time Telemachus was a man, she must marry again**.

And that, she told the suitors, was what she was going to do; although first . . . she just wanted to finish the tapestry she was working on. And that didn't make them very happy, because on the tapestry a massive face was taking shape. And it was the face of her husband. Odysseus, King of Ithaca.

But what Penelope did not know, was that the man
in the tapestry was, at that very moment, walking
along the dusty road towards the palace. Only it
wasn't the same Odysseus who'd set off for Troy
twenty years previously. He was older, his hair was
grey and his face was wrinkled – and also, for now, he
was in disguise.

The Goddess had told him that his wife was a
prisoner in their own home, and that his son was in
danger from suitors who were plotting to take over his
kingdom. So he'd thrown his new boots away, torn his
clothes, coated his arms and legs with mud and
wrapped an old hessian sack round his head so that
only his eyes could be seen. No one would recognize
this dirty, old tramp as Odysseus, the King of Ithaca.

So, as a stranger he returned to his own land.

When he got to the town, he bent his legs, rounded his shoulders and shuffled along. From behind his disguise, he looked at the city he had missed so much. But it was *not* the city he remembered. Its streets were piled with rubbish. There was no music, no laughter, just tired, grey faces with fear in their eyes. The suitors had sucked Ithaca dry.

Then, suddenly, there was singing. But it was not like the singing of old – light and happy, or sad and full of truth. It was lewd, raucous singing, out of tune and out of time, and mainly about rugby . . . And it was coming from the palace. So that's where Odysseus headed. But when he reached it and looked through the big iron gates of his old home, it was not a happy sight. The paint was peeling, the windows were smashed and there was graffiti on the walls and a rubbish tip where the garden had once been. He was starting to get angry when . . .

"On your way!" bawled a beefy, red-faced man in a uniform. "No loitering." A snort of contempt issued from his bulbous, purple nose as he grabbed Odysseus by the scruff of the neck. "Move on filthbag, or I'll tie you up and sell you as a slave!" he shouted, and flung Odysseus into a heap of garbage. Then he broke wind in the tramp's general direction, and stumped off, chuckling to himself.

Now Odysseus was really angry. He lay there, his face and body covered in filth, and rage coursed through him like a swelling bruise. He knew that man. It was Melanthius, the palace butler. Years ago, when he was just a young boy, Odysseus had taught him that every visitor, no matter how humble, must be treated with courtesy. He had clearly forgotten the lesson. Was this really how they treated visitors in Ithaca now? Odysseus hung his head in shame.

But not for long, because at that moment, something licked his face. It was a dog, an old, blind dog with stale breath.

"Clear off!" Odysseus shouted, wiping the spittle from his cheek. But the dog didn't move. It just stood there, panting. Then it drew a rattling, wheezy breath and barked. Odysseus recognized the sound immediately. The old, broken hound in front of him was Argos, the puppy he'd left behind twenty years previously: Argos, the best young hunting dog he'd ever had, who'd saved his life when the wild boar had gashed and scarred his leg the day the whole adventure began.

With tears in his eyes, Odysseus patted and petted the toothless old dog, and threw his arms around its scrawny body. Argos whimpered, wagged his tail, then slowly collapsed into his master's lap and lay still. He was dead. And even though Odysseus' enemies were violating his house, even though his whole being yearned for revenge, he took time to dig a small grave and lay his old friend to rest.

Then slowly Odysseus walked up the overgrown path, pushed open the great, bronze, double doors, and entered his palace.

The Great Hall was crammed full of tables, piled high with food looted from the Ithacan countryside. Carcasses of cows and sheep and pigs, roast duck, roast chicken and roast swan were piled almost to the ceiling; and around the tables, on long wooden benches, were the hundred suitors. Odysseus had seen some horrendous sights in his life, but he'd never seen anything quite as disgusting as this bunch of louts. They were stuffing handfuls of meat into their greedy mouths, snatching chicken legs from each other's grasp, and carelessly overturning vast bowls of steaming vegetables which spread into pools on the table-tops before dripping into great puddles of discarded food on the floor. And between the tables Odysseus' servants waded through the mess, doing the best they could to mop up the slopped food and refill the goblets with wine. But what was the point . . . One suitor picked up a tureen full of soup and poured it over the head of a shivering kitchen-maid. Another pushed a herald's face into a mound of mashed potato and held him there kicking and struggling.

At the door stood Odysseus; his eyes narrowed into slits as he watched the men who were polluting his house. He remembered them all. The two throwing knives at a painting of his mother – he'd been at school with them. The one being sick behind the curtains – that was his second cousin. Oh, they were going to pay for this, they were really going to regret this. But for now . . .

He shuffled around the hall with an old bowl, begging for food, remembering each one of the evil faces which surrounded him. A weaselly one spat in his begging bowl and laughed; a greasy one threw in a chicken bone; one with spots the size of saucers, kicked the bowl from his hand and sent it spinning across the floor. Then a hand grabbed his shoulder and a voice barked "Out!" It was Melanthius, the palace butler, again. "Move!" he shouted, and hit Odysseus across the kidneys with a stubby, black stick. Then, before his victim had time to move away, "*Move!*" he shouted once more, and hit him across the back of his neck.

But this time, Odysseus did not try to move away. Instead, he turned, and smiled, and then snatched the stick from the butler and snapped it in two.

"Oh, look! The old man's angry!" someone giggled.

Then, "Let's make 'em fight!" crowed the weaselly-faced suitor.

"Fight! Fight! Fight! Fight! Fight!" went up the cry and the suitors clustered round in a circle. They were like savages, waiting for a cockfight.

Bets were placed. Money changed hands.

"Two to one he breaks the old man's arms."

"Three to one he tears his eyes out."

"Seven to two he kills him."

No one bet on Odysseus. No one bet on the Greatest Hero of Them All.

"I'm going to enjoy this," said Melanthius, rolling up his sleeves. "I'm going to tear you limb from limb." And he lumbered towards Odysseus, grinning.

A slow handclap started, getting faster and faster. The suitors' eyes glittered in anticipation.

BANG! Suddenly Melanthius wasn't grinning any more. He was lying on his back. His nose was bleeding, one eye was closed, he didn't seem to have any teeth and the tramp was standing over him rubbing his knuckles.

The suitors howled with laughter. "The tramp's the champ!" they chanted and lifted him on their shoulders. Someone tore out a paper crown and crammed it on his head. Someone else started patting him on the back. "But we mustn't let him get too big-headed, must we?" said the slimy, weaselly-faced suitor; and patted him even harder. Then the others joined in, until their pats turned to fists and Odysseus fell to the floor under a heap of punching, giggling, drunken suitors.

"Enough!" A woman's voice stopped them in their tracks.

Penelope strode into the hall, her voice quivering with fury.

"How dare you treat a guest like this! In my house, visitors are treated with respect and courtesy," and although she was a Queen, she took the tramp's hand and drew him to his feet.

"I apologize old man," she said gently. "Please go to my kitchens and eat."

For a moment it seemed as though the old man was going to say something, but then he turned and shuffled out. Then a weaselly voice stopped the Queen in her tracks.

"Penelope, you've been cheating us."

Once more she faced her enemies, like a snowy owl surrounded by stoats.

"You said you'd marry when you finished your

tapestry, but it's been over a month now and it's still not done," continued Prince Weasel.

"I'm a slow worker," replied the Queen.

"No, you're not," retorted Prince Spotty. "Every night you creep downstairs and unpick the previous day's work. Don't try to deny it. Medon the musician spied on you and told us."

Penelope flashed a look at the man who had betrayed her.

"Thank you, Medon," she said coldly, then drew a long, despairing breath. "Very well, I see I can delay no longer. Tomorrow I shall hold a contest. Whoever wins I will marry."

There was silence. Greed and desire filled the faces of the suitors.

"Now go!" she said, and one after another they left the room.

The last to go was Medon. Penelope stopped him at the door.

"How long have you been in the service of this house?" she asked. "Thirty years, isn't it? And yet you could betray me like this."

"I don't get involved, your ladyship," replied the cowardly wretch. "I'm just an entertainer," and he gave an exaggerated, low bow and scampered off after his paymasters.

Penelope sighed a sigh as deep as the sea, then looked up as the tramp shuffled back in from the kitchens.

"We're two of a kind, old man," she said. "They treat me with the same contempt they treat you. Come on, sit down. Your feet are cut and bleeding; the nurse will wash them."

She gestured towards a massive, ruby-studded throne, which sparkled in the flickering torchlight. The tramp moved towards it, but couldn't bring himself to sit down.

"Oh, don't be scared," said Penelope, and drifted away. But it wasn't fear Odysseus was feeling as he once more mounted the ivory step and sat on the throne that had been his and his father's before him. It was a feeling so complicated he didn't have time to sort it out before the old nurse started bustling around his feet with her towel and bowl of water.

"Just pop your tootsies in the suds," she said.

She didn't know what a shock was in store.

"I always say, there's nothing a good scrubbing can't put . . ." She never finished the sentence. At that moment her fingers touched a scar, a long, jagged scar which ran from his ankle to his knee. She gasped, the bowl slipped from her grasp and span and clattered across the floor. In a flash, Odysseus clasped his hand over her mouth and looked around. No one had noticed. The servants were on their hands and knees scrubbing the filth from the floors, the Queen was gazing pensively at her tapestry.

"Yes, it's me," whispered Odysseus. "I have returned. But you must remain silent and pretend not to know me. Speak only to my most trusted servants and tell them to meet me in the courtyard at midnight. Now, send my son to me."

The nurse didn't say a word and her face gave nothing away. But her hand softly squeezed her master's before she silently left the room.

At midnight, Odysseus was standing alone in the Great Hall, when Telemachus burst in.

"I'm sorry you've been treated so badly," he said. "I'm afraid it's the same for all of us and we're simply not powerful enough to do anything about it. But one day, when my father returns, we'll put things to rights. Just you wait. We'll damn well . . ."

Odysseus put his hands on the young man's shoulders and gazed deep into his eyes.

"Telemachus," he said, lifting his hood and showing his face, "don't you know who I am?"

Telemachus stared at the old man, puzzled.

Then he turned and looked at the tapestry his mother had made.

Then back at the tramp.

Then at the tapestry.

Then at the tramp.

"Father!" he whispered, and flung his arms around Odysseus. They hugged each other for a long time, then wiped the tears from each other's eyes.

"Now son," said Odysseus, "we have work to do. Take the shields and javelins off the walls and lock them in the armoury. Tomorrow we take our revenge."

7
Showdown!

Early next morning, the double doors burst open and one hundred suitors poured into the Great Hall, wild with excitement.

But then they skidded to a halt and stared in amazement. In front of them was an axe, with its hilt buried deep in the floor; an axe with a handle the colour of ox-blood and a head of shining silver. And etched on to the head was a one-eyed Cyclops; only where its mouth should have been, there was a gaping hole. And through the hole could be seen another axe with a silver head, and on this one was a hideous gorgon with its mouth wide open, and behind that was another, and another, and another . . . In all, twelve silver axes, one behind the other, in a long line down the entire length of the banqueting hall; each one bearing the face of some hideous monster, and each monster with a yawning hole for a mouth.

And beyond the furthest axe, holding a colossal hunting bow, stood Penelope. Slowly she walked towards the suitors, step by step past the long row of flashing blades. A hush fell on the room, broken only by the sound of her firm footsteps. She had no idea how the day would end, she only knew that her hatred for these men was total. Her eyes took in everything; the suitors slavering with anticipation, her son biting his nails in the corner, and in the shadow of the hearth the old tramp, barely visible under his hessian hood.

When she re ⌐ the first axe, she stopped and spoke.

"This bow belonged to my husband, Odysseus. No one, save he, has ever been able to put it to use. Whoever can fire a single arrow from it so that it passes through the holes in these twelve axes, that man I will marry."

There was a moment's silence, then a whoop of laughter as the suitors raced towards her and ripped the bow from her hands. It was going to be a doddle and everyone wanted to go first.

"Wait!" she ordered. "My son shall make the first attempt. If Telemachus succeeds, I will marry no one, but will remain a widow until the end of my days."

The suitors hissed as Telemachus stepped forward and took his father's ancient weapon. He placed an arrow on the bowstring and pulled. But it wouldn't budge an inch. It felt as though it had been made for a giant. Sweat burst out on his forehead, his muscles quivered with the strain, and then s l o w l y the bow began to bend, when . . . BEDUNG! It snapped back into place. Once more he tried and BEDUNG! once more he failed. The third time he took a deep breath and in his mind's eye he visualized the arrow speeding towards its target. He knew he could do it! He closed one eye, he took aim, he began to pull the bowstring back . . . and at that moment the tramp gently shook his head. No one else noticed, but Telemachus knew what to do.

BEDUNG! the bow snapped into place again.

"It's no good mother," he sighed. "I'm not strong enough."

Penelope's eyes darkened, but she said nothing.

"My turn," hissed the weaselly faced suitor and snatched the bow.

He pulled.

Nothing happened. Quite literally nothing. Although he pulled so hard his weasel face went bright purple and his eyes popped out like radishes, the bow didn't move a hair's breadth.

The suitors hooted in derision.

"Now me," whined the pimply suitor.

But once again, despite an effort that led to two burst blood vessels . . . complete failure.

Then another suitor, so greedy that he kept a permanent, greasy napkin dangling from his neck, tried his luck.

His clammy fingers wrapped themselves around the dark wood of the old bow and he started to yank and tug at it. Penelope watched his pathetic fumblings and didn't know whether to laugh or cry.

"Perhaps the string needs greasing," yelled someone and threw a slimy lump of meat fat at him.

"Or moistening," suggested someone else, pouring a plate of soup over his head.

The greedy slob gave one final heave, slipped on the soup and crashed into a table. Food, drink and suitors went flying. There were hysterical howls of laughter as more and more men waded through the mess, falling over each other as they attempted, fruitlessly, to get to the bow.

Behind his hood, Odysseus said nothing. Only his eyes moved. His trusted servants were in position; there were no weapons on the walls; everything was ready.

Meanwhile the suitors lay on the floor, kicking their

legs and sniggering helplessly among the broken bottles. But their laughter suddenly died away.

"Wait a minute," said the pimply suitor. "Perhaps it isn't possible to bend the bow at all. Perhaps its another trick to get rid of us."

"Yes," hissed the weasel. "Perhaps we ought to make our own decision, now."

"Your Noble Highnesses, may *I* try?" asked Odysseus softly.

"You? You're just a tramp," scoffed the weasel.

"He's as good a man as any here," replied the Queen. "Old man, take the bow."

Odysseus turned it in his hands and felt its weight. Then he softly plucked the bowstring. A long, low note rang out and reverberated around the hall.

"Please leave now, Mother," said Telemachus quietly.

Penelope looked at her son, puzzled.

"Trust me," he urged.

She smiled, then turned and left. For the first time in his life, her son had spoken with the determination of a grown man.

And now Odysseus rested his arrow against the bowstring and smiled. The secret wasn't strength, of course. He was a trickster, not a great ape. He simply placed his foot on the base of the bow and with a flick of his wrists the bow was bent and at his shoulder. The suitors gasped, but he didn't let it break his concentration. He thought back to his hunting days, to those countless arrows speeding towards their prey.

"Always concentrate on your target," his grandfather had told him when he was a lad. "Anything nearer will look after itself."

113

So Odysseus fixed his eyes on the far wall, on a tiny dribble of wine just visible through the twelve holes in the axes. He felt the arrow's feathers against his cheek, he felt the taut bowstring aching to be released, he stared long and hard at the wine stain, then he let go the arrow and WHOOSH!

Straight through the gaping hole in the Cyclops it flew.

Through the gorgon.

Through the harpy.

Through the mouths of all twelve monsters, until VDUNG! It embedded itself deep in the wall. Right in the middle of that dribble of wine.

The suitors stared, dumbstruck. But then there was the chink of coins as the weaselly one tossed a purse at Odysseus' feet.

"You were lucky," he said. "Now go."

But Odysseus didn't move. Instead he looked deep into the weasel's eyes, and whispered – the loudest whisper they'd ever heard – the last whisper they'd ever hear. "Gentlemen – the hour has come."

Immediately BERDANG! The big, double doors slammed shut.

BERDANG! BERDANG! The windows slammed shut too; and outside, the sound of a few, trusty servants could be heard, lashing them tight. No one could get in or out.

Then CHUNK! Telemachus threw a quiver full of arrows to his father, and Odysseus scattered them on the floor in front of him.

"We underestimated you," said the pimply suitor, his voice edged with fear. "I drink your health." He lifted his goblet, but he never drank. Odysseus' arrow went through his throat like a hot knife through butter. He slumped on to the table, his dead head resting on a pig with an orange in its mouth.

"Kill him!" yelled the suitors, and rushed to the wall for the weapons. But the shields and javelins which had always hung there had disappeared.

Then a voice behind them froze them where they stood. "You terrorized my wife. You ruined my country. You plundered my house. You abused my servants. Now prepare to die."

Slowly, slowly, they turned to see who it was who had so confidently condemned them to death. At first they thought it was just the tramp, and their spirits rose an inch or two. But then the tramp tore off his hood, and their spirits sank a mile. Because in front of them stood Odysseus, King of Ithaca. He was home at last, after twenty years. And he was very angry.

The colour drained from the suitors' faces and the weaselly suitor dropped to his knees. "Odysseus," he squealed, "we've behaved abominably. I'm truly, truly sorry. Gosh, I'm sorry. I mean, so incredibly sorry . . . really, really sorry. But, hey, welcome home."

Then he stood up, and stepped towards Odysseus, stretching forth a hand of friendship. Or at least, it would have been a hand of friendship, if it hadn't contained a tiny knife he'd just cunningly taken from his boot as he knelt. Unluckily for him, it was the last cunning thing he'd ever try. Two seconds later, he had an arrow through his forehead. Odysseus wasn't in the mood for shaking hands.

ZZZIIINNGGG! A hundred swords suddenly shot from a hundred scabbards, and the rest of the suitors, knowing it was them or him, charged Odysseus. But the man they were charging had blinded the Cyclops, he had overcome the Sirens, he had braved the twin horrors of Scylla and Charybdis. They didn't stand a chance. Slowly but surely Odysseus advanced until, in desperation, the suitors overturned the tables and dived for cover.

But it wasn't cover for long. Now Telemachus and a few trusty servants joined Odysseus, and one by one, the suitors breathed their last. They tried charging, but each time they were pushed back as arrow after arrow sent them off to Hell. What a day this would be for the Fat Batsman. A hundred new arrivals from his old home town! Odysseus was winning, and it looked as though nothing could stop him, until suddenly he realised he'd made one miscalculation. His arrows were running out.

"Quick, son," he ordered Telemachus. "Slip out to the armoury while I hold them off."

Telemachus edged round the side wall, over dead bodies and scared kitchen-maids and through a tiny door in the corner. Hoping that no one had followed him, he shot down the corridor and, taking a small gold key from his pocket, he opened the door to the armoury at the end of it. Seconds later he returned with an armful of arrows.

"Well done," said Odysseus. "These should do the trick." But they didn't. The suitors held on.

"Something's wrong," said Odysseus. "Just take a look at the armoury again."

So once more, Telemachus crept out of the door in the corner and into the corridor. And he found the answer. There in front of him stood the butler

Melanthius, his arms full of arrows for the suitors and a tiny gold key swinging from his key chain.

"Oh, dear," said Telemachus calmly.

"Oh, no!" whined Melanthius pitifully, and sank to the floor as Telemachus' knife entered his stomach.

Back in the Great Hall the old nurse was passing out arrows to Odysseus and his men. "Collect all the loyal servants who aren't fighters," whispered Odysseus, "and lead them to safety."

Swiftly, the old woman moved around the hall touching first this servant and then that and then led them through the tiny door.

Medon, the treacherous musician, tiptoed after them, till he felt a heavy hand on his shoulder.

"Where are you going?" asked Odysseus.

"Oh, just along. I didn't really do anything wrong you know," laughed Medon nervously. "I'm just an entertainer. All I ever wanted was to make people laugh."

"Unfortunately," replied Odysseus, "even a clown must choose which side he's on. And you chose wrong."

Medon giggled, slipped on a stupid false nose and began to sing a comic song. "Don't tell me about my mother-in-law, she's as ugly as a . . ."

But no one ever discovered how ugly she was. Odysseus picked him up and hurled him back into the room. He died on the uplifted sword of an oncoming suitor.

And now it was time for father and son to make the final charge. The final end to the shame that had hung like a dirty storm-cloud over Ithaca for ten years. They wrenched the twelve silver axes from the

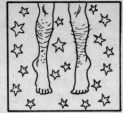

ground and, whirling them round their heads, flung
them at the enemy. Twelve silver blades shot in
twelve different directions, and twelve heads were cut
from twelve bodies. Again and again the blades
flashed until, at last, it was over. The cloud was
gone.

"Open the doors," ordered Odysseus, the
reinstated King of Ithaca, and in an instant the
blinding sun burst into the banqueting hall.

Smiling with relief, but gasping with exhaustion,
the trusty servants leant on their weapons, listening to
the silence broken only by the drip! drip! drip! of an
overturned flask of wine. Odysseus himself staggered
outside and fell on to a wooden bench. Above him he
saw the sky, clear and blue, except for a solitary,
white cloud. And for an instant he was sure he could
see, deep within it, the smiling face of the Goddess –
then she was gone for ever. Sitting up once more, he
looked over the city and on up to the high hills of
Ithaca. At last they felt like they were his again. This
was the land he had fought for, and now there could
be peace. After twenty years he could finally rest.

Then a voice spoke from behind his shoulder.

"Is it really you?"

He turned and saw Penelope. And he nodded.

But she did not move, and she didn't smile.

"How can I be sure? The Odysseus who left me twenty years ago was young and in his prime. The man I see now has grey hair."

"Those are tricks that time plays on the best of us," said Odysseus quietly. "It *is* me."

But Penelope still hesitated. "Well, maybe. Give me time to think. Sleep out here tonight. I'll bring your bed into the courtyard."

"How will you do that?" asked Odysseus, smiling. "Our bed is carved from a living olive tree. Will you pull it up by its roots?"

That was all the proof she needed. In the quiet, calm of the evening a King and his Queen, both no longer young, clung tight to each other, like drowning sailors clinging to a rock. They'd survived.

Later, Odysseus left the city and climbed up into the hills. Ahead of him was what had once been a stately old house, but now its roof had collapsed and the door was off its hinges. He hid behind a battered fence and looked on in tears. Working in the garden was his father. The last time Odysseus had seen him, he was a noble king, but the suitors had stripped him of his riches and now he looked like an old scarecrow, with a battered hat, holes in his shoes, gloves without fingers and shaking hands.

"Who's there?" the old man demanded, squinting through the rickety fencing.

"Good afternoon," replied Odysseus smoothly. "I'm a travelling salesman from Lemnos. I've got an excellent range of javelins. Perhaps your son would like to sample one?"

"Go away!" snapped his father. "I had a son, the finest in the land, but he's dead."

"That's what you think," said Odysseus with a smile. "Father."

"You?" muttered the shaky old man and staggered towards him.

But when he got closer, he stopped. "No! Never! You're not Odysseus. The old Odysseus was bigger than you."

"Well, maybe, but I've still got the scar on my leg."

"You could have faked it. No, you're too old."

Odysseus had forgotten how stubborn his father could be. "Look," he said firmly, "do you see that blackberry bush?"

"Yes," answered his father grumpily.

"Well, you planted that the day I was born, *and*

those plum trees. And there were blackcurrants over there. What's happened to them?"

"They got leaf curl and died," said his father. "Welcome home, son. Why are you selling javelins?"

As the shadows lengthened, father and son looked across their kingdom — at the fishing villages, the white-washed cottages, the tiny boats, and the farmers going in for their tea. And Odysseus thought back to the Trojan War. All those wasted lives. And he thought back to his hellish journey home. All those wasted years. His life had passed by, his youth gone. The Greatest Hero of Them All, yes indeed. But, oh, at what a price.

"Oh, come on, don't get broody," said his Dad. "It's time for dinner. Welcome home."

And drawing his great sword of war for the last time, Odysseus flung it into the bushes and set off down the hill to start again.

Some other exciting titles from Knight Books which
you might enjoy:

EDWARD BLISHEN

ROBIN HOOD

"We are all outlaws now. But we are not thieves. No
good man need ever fear us. Now together we must
swear an oath. We must swear to harm no one who has
harmed no other. We must swear to fight whatever is
evil and cruel. And our solemnest oath must be to pro-
tect the poor, and whoever's been wronged."

And so began the thrilling story of Robin Hood, the
most famous outlaw the world has ever known.

KNIGHT BOOKS

ANTHONY HOPE

THE PRISONER OF ZENDA

"God save the King!
God save the King!"

As I swallowed the last drop of my cup of coffee the bells throughout all the city broke out into a joyful peal, and the sound of a military band and of men cheering smote upon my ear

"God save the King!"

Colonel Sapt's mouth wrinkled into a smile. "God save 'em both!" he whispered.

The classic tale of treachery, bravery – and substitution!

KNIGHT BOOKS

J. MEADE FALKNER

MOONFLEET

"In returning to the vault, I had no very sure purpose in mind; only a vague surmise that this finding of Blackbeard's coffin would somehow lead to the finding of his treasure."

Although he does not realise it at the time, John Trenchard's visit to a dank and dismal vault beneath the local church does provide the vital clue to the discovery of some fabulous hidden treasure. But everything is far from straightforward and John's curiosity almost costs him his life. It also causes his involvement with a gang of smugglers and leads him into a series of thrilling adventures as he sets off in search of Blackbeard's treasure.

KNIGHT BOOKS